Lynnell,
Hope you
the story! I appr
you buying my book
Blessings.
Darlia

A Home For Her Heart
A Spinster Orphan Train novella
Darlia Sawyer

Copyright © 2017
Written by: Darlia Sawyer
Published by: Forget Me Not Romances, a division of
Winged Publications

ISBN-10:1545591997

ISBN-13:9781545591994

Thank you for your love, unwavering support and endless hours of help, Ken Sawyer.

Thank you for your friendship and for making this better, Patti Hill.

Chapter One

1891

Tears spilled down Ella's cheeks as Anna Wilson helped her step off the orphan train in Longview, Texas. She embraced the twelve-year-old girl. "What's wrong, Ella? Are you tired? I would understand if you were. We've traveled to so many towns in the last several weeks."

Ella wiped tears from her eyes. "No one wants me."

"I'm trying my best to find homes for each of you. You all deserve to have the love of a family." Anna hugged the six children in her care. "I have a good feeling about today. The last agent said several families were waiting for the next orphan train."

Anna noticed Ella's flushed cheeks "Ella, you look warm. Are you running a temperature?"

"I don't think so." Ella pulled at the front of her dress. "It's hot."

"This Texas humidity is suffocating." Anna laid her hand on Ella's forehead. "You're not running a temperature. I hope the people today understand what gifts each of you are. We're late, let's go find the opera house."

Anna followed the six children along the wooden sidewalk. Ella's red curls bounced with each step she took. Dust engulfed them from the passing horses and wagons. Michael coughed. *Did anyone ever get used to all this dirt?* Anna understood now why they covered the streets in New York with brick. It made walking so much easier. They passed by a bakery and the aroma of homemade bread made Anna's mouth water.

"I'm hungry. Can we buy sweet rolls, Miss Wilson?" Sam asked.

"I wish we had time. They smell wonderful." Anna spotted the opera house across the street. "We're almost there."

Anna opened the door of a two-story brick building and they walked in. Their train had arrived an hour late, and there were around twenty people waiting for them. There were more women than men sitting in groups and talking. A middle-aged man in a black suit came toward them.

"Welcome. I'm Pastor Williams and we've been expecting you." He held his hand out to Anna. "Did everyone have a pleasant trip?" He didn't wait for the children to respond. He asked Anna. "Are you comfortable introducing yourself?"

She shook his hand. "Yes to both questions and thank you. Children, please go sit in the chairs they've set out on stage."

Anna followed the children down the aisle, admiring the stained-glass windows of the Longview Opera House. There were four long windows on each side, and they cast shades of yellow, red, green and blue on the wooden floor in a kaleidoscope of colors. Each window depicted a scene from a famous play. It reminded Anna of the church her parents attended when she was a little girl. She hadn't been to church since then. Grief caught Anna by surprise and she had a difficult time holding back tears. Her parents had died eight years ago.

Her heart broke for each child on stage. Most of them had never known their parents, and the rest had lost theirs at a young age. The orphanage had provided the girls with white dresses, stockings, shoes and a bow for her hair. The four boys had on white shirts, jackets, knee pants, hats, socks and shoes. They looked adorable. Their sole possessions included one more outfit and a Bible.

Anna stepped to the front of the stage. She no longer got nervous speaking in front of people. Her concern for the children pushed her to overcome the anxiousness she used to feel.

"I want to thank everyone for coming. My name is Anna Wilson. I am an agent for the Children's Aid Society in New York City. We have traveled many miles to find families who will love these children. I care about each of them."

"They listen well and are considerate and loving. In the past, many people thought it appropriate to treat orphans as servants. I won't allow this." Anna glared at the audience. "I hope you'll love them as your own. Most of them were living on the streets before someone took them to the Children's Aid Society. They'd lost one or both parents and often their siblings. Their lives have been filled with difficulties and sorrow. My hope is you'll find it a privilege to provide a home for them. In return they'll show you how much it means to be a part of your family."

"When I finish speaking, I hope you'll talk with each child. I have a few rules," Anna studied the crowd. "I don't allow anyone to touch their muscles or look at their teeth. They're all healthy. Agents used to allow this, but I won't. They need respect. If you're interested in a child, I'll check with Longview's community leaders to find out if they believe your family would provide a good home. The children must feel comfortable around you, so I'll watch how you communicate and connect with them." She cleared her throat. "Could we get a drink of water? We had a long train ride and we're not used to this heat."

Pastor Williams left and returned with a bucket of water and a ladle.

"Thank you." Anna let the children drink first. She wished they had ice for the warm water, but it eased her parched throat.

"I'd like to introduce everyone. Children, please step forward when I say your name. First is Sam Foster, he's twelve." A lanky brown haired boy took his place by Anna. "A family in Opelousas, Louisiana took his younger brother Ben. They didn't have room for both boys. Sam has Ben's address so he can write to him. He wants to visit him one day. Their parents died in a factory fire. When Sam was eight and Ben was five, someone found them on the streets and brought them to the orphanage."

"Next is Ella Murphey, she's twelve." Ella stood next to Sam. She was taller than him and her red curls stuck out in every direction. Her cheeks grew pink which caused her freckles to appear darker. "Ella helps with the little ones. I don't know what I would've done without her. She doesn't remember her family. Her father brought her to the orphanage when she was three."

"Then we have Matthew, he's ten." He tried to go on the opposite side of Miss Wilson but Ella grabbed his arm and pulled him beside her. Matthew frowned at Ella but recovered quickly and turned toward the audience and smiled, causing dimples to appear in his chubby cheeks. "His parents and siblings died from typhoid. A couple found him huddled in a corner of the apartment building they'd lived in and took him to the orphanage."

Anna motioned to the small blonde-haired girl to stand next to her. "Laura is eight. When her parents didn't return from a voyage to England, her grandmother cared for her. No one ever heard what happened to her parents. When her grandmother died Laura was only four. A family friend brought her to the orphanage."

"Last are five-year-old twins, Scott and Michael." They ran next to Laura. Each brother a mirror image of the other, black short hair, bright blue eyes and two missing top teeth. "If you're thinking about taking them, I hope you'll take both. Twins have a special connection. Their mother left them on the steps of the orphanage when they were babies. She'd pinned a note stating their names, and that she had no other choice. Thank you, children, you can sit down. Does anyone have questions before you talk with them?" Anna watched a man get up and walk out. He wore torn jean overalls, and a ripped shirt. She wondered how often he bathed as there were dirt smudges across his face.

A woman with thick glasses stood up as she squinted at Anna. "If you're not married can you care for a child?"

Anna scanned the crowd. She guessed most of them to be in their late twenties or early thirties, including the woman asking the question. "We prefer you're married, but if you want to care for a child, we're willing to let you try."

A man in a gray vest, jacket, matching trousers and black top hat stood, "Do you check on each child after they go with a family? What if a child is unhappy and doesn't want to stay in your home? Or if the families realize they can't care for them, how would you resolve it?"

"Yes, agents check on the children each time they bring new orphans. I'll be here for two weeks to make sure they're adjusting well and to make sure children from previous orphan trains are doing well. The agent after me should do the same. If a child is unhappy, we find another family for them. If we can't, we take them back to the Children's Aid Society in New York City. Children have run away from homes, and we've never heard from them again. We often learn afterward that those children were being physically or emotionally mistreated." Anna patted Scott's shoulder as he hopped from one foot to the other.

An older woman in the back row covered her mouth with her gloved hand. "Oh my, who would do such awful things?"

"Sometimes a neighbor or family member will do things in the privacy of their home you'd never imagine. I hope if you notice or hear something bad happening in a family, you'll report it. I'm glad most problems we have aren't so awful and are easily worked out." Anna paused and tucked a few loose strands of her toffee brown hair behind her ear. "Anyone else?" No one spoke. "If you come up with other questions, I'd love to answer them. Thank you for coming."

Anna paced the stage as people came to talk with the children. It'd be difficult to let any of the children go. She'd come to love them. She walked over and stood in front of the curtain on the right side of the stage. She needed to get her emotions under control. Anna heard whispering behind her.

"Mary, what about the two girls?" A hoarse voice asked.

Anna noticed a hole in the curtain. She could see two older women through it.

"I'm not sure about the little girl, Bertha. The taller girl with red hair appears adequate." Mary glanced at the girls. "No one is saying anything to her, so you might be her only opportunity."

"I don't have time for nonsense. I need someone to do the housework I can no longer do. My health makes it difficult for me. I'm too old to take care of a child." Bertha sat in a wooden chair. It groaned and creaked beneath her. "She would have to follow my rules."

"Bertha, if she's in school, she can only help you in the evenings. And all children misbehave. I wonder if you have sufficient patience to have a child around, even an older one. Maybe this isn't the best solution for you." Mary sat next to her, clutching a big bag to her bosom.

"She doesn't need more school. She'll get real life

Darlia Sawyer

experience taking care of a home. If she marries, she will need to know household management." Bertha scooted back in her chair, a snap caused her to stand abruptly, as the chair broke into pieces all over the floor. "They sure don't make chairs like they used to."

Anna had heard enough. She went around the curtain. "I overheard your conversation, and I won't let Ella leave with you. As I expressed in my introduction, they're not servants. They need love and a family. Ella is a lovely and helpful girl. She deserves more than someone who wants a housekeeper. You should both leave."

"Of all the nerve. Mary, let's go." Bertha's face turned red. "The mayor will hear about this. I wanted to help that child, and this is how I'm treated." Bertha waddled down the stairs, huffing and puffing her way through the people and out the door. Mary followed behind her.

Anna's heart raced as she walked back to the front of the stage. Her nails dug into her palms as she clenched her hands into fists. Her cheeks were on fire and she knew her face was red. *I can't believe how selfish people are. Ella deserves a real family.*

The well-dressed man who had asked the questions earlier approached Anna. He was holding hands with an attractive woman. "Miss Wilson, my name is Thomas Gage, and this is my wife, Emma." He shook Anna's hand. "We're interested in providing a home for the twins. In our five years of marriage we haven't been blessed with children. Our home is nice and we have four bedrooms. I'm the town doctor and my wife would stay with them."

Anna drew a deep breath. "I appreciate you wanting

8

to provide a home for them but are you aware of how rambunctious two little boys can be? They might destroy something valuable. If you had children of your own, would you still want the twins? Or would they be a burden to you?" Anna glared at Mrs. Gage.

"Oh no, Miss Wilson, we'd think of the boys as ours." Mrs. Gage paused. "They'd be the older siblings to any child we might have. Once you give a child your heart, you wouldn't take it back. I assure you, God gives us enough love for everyone in our lives." She clutched her husband's hand as if clinging to a lifeline.

"I wonder if God bothers with such matters. He allowed their parents to give them away." Anna took a few deep breaths, to calm herself down. "I'm sorry if I sound cynical. Before I came over here, I overheard a conversation which upset me. My recommendation would be to take Michael and Scott for two hours today. When you're done, bring them to our hotel and you can do the same for the next few days. You could increase the time you have them each day. As long as everything goes well for the twins and both of you, we'll talk about a permanent arrangement." Anna smiled.

Mrs. Gage's expression softened. "Oh, what a wonderful idea. It'd give us time to get our home prepared." She glanced up at her husband. "What do you think, Thomas?"

"It's a good plan. We'll get to know them and they can decide if they want to live with us. Would it be all right if we took them to lunch and to our house to play? We have a large yard and a new furry puppy." Mr. Gage lifted his hat and wiped his forehead with a handkerchief.

"Let me talk with the boys. I'll be right back." Anna walked over to Michael and Scott. "There's a couple who wishes to have lunch with you both. After eating they'll take you to their home to play with their new puppy for a while. Would you like to go with them?"

"Yes, Miss Wilson," Michael gave her a toothless smile.

Scott nodded. "I would love to play with a puppy."

"When you are through playing, they'll bring you to the hotel. You'll have lots of fun." Anna walked back with the boys to give the good news to Mr. and Mrs. Gage.

~

"Well girls, let's eat supper and find our hotel. Our luggage should be there." Anna took each girl by the hand. "I can't say I'm sorry the right family didn't come for you both. Now I have more time with you. We'll stay here for two weeks. Our next and last stop will be in Nacogdoches, Texas. I believe families are waiting there for both of you."

"It's all right Miss Wilson. No one wants me. They don't even speak to me. I'll go back to the orphanage with you." Ella wiped tears away.

"No one wants me either. They only take boys. I'm happy Sam, Matthew and the twins found families but why don't they like girls, Miss Wilson?" Laura looked up at Anna with her big blue eyes brimming with unshed tears. "Doesn't God want us to find a family?"

Anna's heart broke. The girls' lives had been full of disappointments. Every time she paraded them in front of families, their hopes were high they'd find a home. When they didn't, rejection and disappointment settled on them.

Anna understood their responses. She'd experienced pain when the man she'd loved rejected her for someone else. At twenty-nine her prospects of finding love were slim. She resented the label of spinster, but it applied to her. Anna wanted a family but how could she ever trust a man with her heart again?

She needed a plan to take care of these precious girls. Ella's chances of someone wanting her for more than a housekeeper or nanny weren't good, as Anna had witnessed today. Laura wasn't as old, but girls weren't valued as highly as boys. The West needed laborers. Boys grew up and helped on the homesteads.

"Oh girls, you're beautiful. If the right family comes along, they'll love you as much as I do. I'm certain God wants you both to find families. Why wouldn't He? You're angels. After supper let's eat ice cream. It's been a long day and you both deserve a treat." Anna bent and wiped the tears away and kissed them on the cheek. "No more crying. It's time for fun."

Ella hugged Anna tight. "I wish we could stay with you, Miss Wilson."

"Me too." Laura joined in the hug.

"Me too." Anna whispered to herself.

~

The rocking rhythm of the train lolled Ella and Laura to sleep for most of the journey from Longview to Nacogdoches, Texas. Anna enjoyed looking out the window as forests and lakes sped by. She caught a whiff of coffee brewing in the dining car. Her stomach rumbled.

"Next stop Nacogdoches. Please prepare to disembark." The conductor announced.

Being an agent gave Anna the ability to travel and

see places, but it didn't pay enough for her to live on her own. Maybe she should check into getting a teaching certificate and moving out West with the girls to teach.

Screeches and squeals from the train brakes startled Anna from her thoughts, and she looked outside at the depot coming into view.

Ella sat up, rubbing her eyes. "Are we there?"

"I believe so. We'll pick up our baggage and go to the hotel. I didn't know when we'd arrive when I sent out the telegram, so we won't be meeting with families until tomorrow." Anna stood. The girls followed her down the aisle.

"What a beautiful town." Anna glanced around at the small crowd as she stepped off the train. The smell of pine filled the air and evergreen trees stood as strong sentinels overlooking the area.

"It's pretty, Miss Wilson, so many trees. It's hot here too, but I like it. There's lots of shade." Ella stepped off the train.

Anna helped Laura down the steps. "Do you like it?"

"I do." Laura grabbed Ella's hand and smiled. "We'll meet our families here, Ella."

Ella stared at the ground. "You will, Laura."

"We need to get our luggage and find the hotel." Anna stepped backward and tripped over a satchel on the ground behind her. She tried regaining her balance, but instead strong arms wrapped around her waist. However, they didn't stop her fall. She landed on top of a muscular man.

"Oh my," Anna tried to push herself up. *Where should she place her hands so she wouldn't touch the man underneath her?* Her cheeks were on fire and people were starring.

"Miss Wilson, are you okay? That sure was funny," Ella giggled. "Grab my hands and I'll pull you up."

Anna made it to her feet and straightened her skirt. She turned around to thank the man who broke her fall. He wore jeans, brown cowboy boots and a white shirt. Dark brown hair waved from under his white cowboy hat. When she found the courage to look into his face, a pair of ice-blue eyes looked amused at her embarrassment. "I'm so sorry. I didn't check behind me before I backed up," she stammered. "Did I hurt you?"

"I'm fine, miss. Someone as slim as you wouldn't hurt me. I tried catching you but it didn't go as intended. Are you all right?" He held out his hand. "My name is, Joshua."

Anna shook his hand. "I'm Anna Wilson and nothing is hurt, thanks to you. Glad you didn't hurt your head or break anything."

Joshua picked up the satchel. "It's dented. Is it yours?"

"It isn't. I wonder who'd sit a bag down and walk off?" Anna scanned the crowd, but no one rushed to claim the satchel. "I guess we should leave it, in case they come back. Do you know if they're unloading the luggage yet?"

Joshua sat the satchel on the ground. "We can find out. I need to get my mother's trunks. Follow me and I'll load your bags into your wagon."

"Oh, I wouldn't want to bother you with our bags. I'm sure you're busy, and we don't have a wagon. I'll hire someone to take our bags to the Grand Hotel." Anna took the girl's hands. "We'll follow you, though."

"It's no problem. I'll load your bags into my wagon and drop them off at the hotel. Which ones are yours? I'd offer you all a ride, but I'm out of room. My mother is coming to live with me and she brought enough trunks to fill two wagons. Which won't leave space for young ladies, sorry to say."

Anna tried to keep up with him. "Please don't bother about us. The girls and I like to walk. We'll get to see part of the town."

Joshua walked toward the men unloading luggage from the train to the wooden platform. He found his mother's trunks while Anna and the girls searched for theirs.

"We sat our luggage over there." Anna pointed to the bags. "Thank you again for helping us."

"You're welcome." Joshua smiled.

Anna's breath caught. Joshua had dimples, and his smile made her pulse pick up a beat or two. "Where is the Grand Hotel?"

"Turn right at the end of this street. It's three blocks down Main Street to the left. Have a good day ladies. It's nice to meet you." Joshua grabbed the bags.

"It was nice meeting you as well. Let's find the hotel, girls." Anna walked away but couldn't help taking one last glance at her rescuer. He was watching them. Their eyes met. Anna turned back around. *I'm sure he's married and has a family.*

She needed to accept her life. Her days would be filled with finding a home for the girls and checking on the children from previous orphan trains. Who had time for men, even the kind and handsome cowboy type men? He'd only end up breaking her heart.

Chapter Two

"We're home Mother." Joshua hopped off the wagon and helped Clara down.

She took in all that was different and the same. "The ranch hasn't changed much. It seems like it was only yesterday I said goodbye, instead of twelve years. You've done a great job keeping the buildings repaired. I even see a few new ones. Your father worked hard to keep it looking nice."

Clara walked up the front porch steps of the white two-story farmhouse. A small table stood between two rocking chairs and a porch swing hung next to them. The other side of the porch had children's toys scattered about. Four round columns held up the roof over the porch. "You added a swing Joshua, I tried to get your father to make one numerous times, but he insisted our rocking chairs were enough. What other changes have you made?"

"Before Sarah passed away, we added onto the back porch so the mud would stay out of the house. She would get upset if I tracked dirt in on her clean floors.

The back porch is the same size as the front." Joshua grabbed a trunk from the wagon bed and followed her inside.

"I'm sorry Sarah's gone. You loved her a lot, Joshua. We all did. We were glad your sister, Lizzy decided to help you after Sarah passed. I don't know how you've dealt with the ranch, three children and mourning your Sarah. Your father would be proud of all you've accomplished, as am I." Clara stood at the bottom of the staircase. "I'll stay in a bedroom upstairs. I can manage the stairs a few times a day." Clara chuckled. "When we built the house we wanted each of you to have your own rooms. It reduced the bickering amongst the six of you."

"Mother, you're here." Lizzie walked into the entry and hugged Clara.

"I've missed you." Clara pushed a few loose wisps of Lizzy's light brown hair from her face. "Your hair is so long."

"I haven't cut it in three years. I'm happy you're here to help with the wedding and with the children. It helps me feel better about moving out. The wedding's in a week. I can't believe I'll be a wife and have a home." Lizzy blushed.

"I'm thrilled for you. The children will miss you. You've been their aunt and mother the last two years and the only mother Emily has known. It's won't be easy for them to adjust to you not living here. They've been through so much. I'm thankful they've had a wonderful father and aunt to love them." Clara smiled at her son and daughter. "What smells so delicious?"

"I have beef stew simmering for dinner. Bread is rising for rolls and I made an apple pie. It's ready for the oven. I wanted to welcome you home with a meal like you used to prepare for us." Lizzy dusted flour off her apron.

"I'm impressed. The house is tidy, delicious food is cooking and not a peep from any of the children." Clara peeked into the living room. "It's all as I remember. It's nice to see my parents' furniture still getting use. They were so proud of what they brought from England. The lace curtains are new. This room has always been my favorite. Where *are* my grandchildren?"

"The girls are down for naps. Seth is outside helping Jake plant the garden. He wants to do everything the men do." Lizzy wiped her forehead with the back of her hand. "It's getting warm for the first of May."

Joshua lumbered up the stairs. "Can we talk later? This trunk is heavy. Follow me upstairs, Mother, and we'll figure out a room for you."

"Why don't you share my room, Mother? I'll be moving out in a week. We'll have extra time to catch up once everyone's in bed." Lizzy climbed the stairs.

Clara followed Lizzy up the stairs. "Sharing a room is an excellent idea. It'll be fun to catch up. You've been gone two years Lizzy, and I want to hear about the man you're marrying."

"If I didn't carry the trunks up for you, Mother, you and Lizzy wouldn't even remember I'm here." Joshua sat the trunk in Lizzy's bedroom.

"We'd never forget you, Joshua. I won't have much time to catch up with your sister. I'm glad she will only be living twenty miles away." Clara looked around the room.

"I understand, I wanted to give you both a hard

time. It's good you have a chance to be together before the wedding. I could never thank Lizzy enough for all she's done to help." Joshua winked at his sister.

"Aww... you both are making me feel so good. Let's get you settled in, Mother." Lizzy opened the first trunk.

~

"I see you two have made yourself comfortable." Joshua walked up the porch steps and sat down in a rocking chair where Lizzy and Clara rested in the gathering darkness with the children.

Clara yawned and laid her head back on the wooden slats of the porch swing. "The fragrance from the roses is intoxicating, so sweet. I used to love sitting outside with your father after dinner when the work was finished. It's my favorite time of day. The crickets chirping their own special song. It's so peaceful."

"Slipping out here for some quiet after a long day has been a blessing." Lizzy rocked Emily. "I'm sure you're tired, Mother. You've had a long day."

"I love having grandchildren to cuddle, but I am a little drowsy. I'll rock myself to sleep before these two close their eyes." Clara put one arm around Rebecca and the other around Seth. "When do I get to meet your soon-to-be husband, Lizzy?"

"Mark has been adding onto our ranch house, but he'll be here tomorrow evening for dinner. He wanted to give us a night to catch up without him. Emily's asleep, I think I'll put her in bed." Lizzy wrapped the quilt tighter around Emily and went into the house.

Clara spread a blanket over her and the children's laps against the chilled air of a Texas evening. She turned to Joshua. "What do you think about Lizzy's fiancée?"

"Mark Arris is the hardest worker I've ever had on the ranch. Most of what you see as improvements here he helped us with the last three years. I would have kept him on forever, but he had his own dream to follow, and I sure wouldn't stand in his way. He used an inheritance to buy Samuel Johnson's place. He took a piece of land no one wanted and is building it into a good cattle ranch.

"All in all, I like the man fine, except that he's taking my little sister away. She's been a blessing for me and the children." Joshua cleared his throat. He couldn't get too emotional or he might shed a few tears. "We'll miss her. He'll make a decent husband. If not I'll be paying him a visit."

"Lizzy told me most of this in her letters but it's good to hear it from you too. I'm reassured because you think he's the right man for her." Clara moved Rebecca's head to her lap as she'd fallen sound asleep.

"Let's all get some sleep. Every day on the ranch is long. Joshua, will you carry Rebecca? I think Seth and I can make it upstairs ourselves." Clara winked at her grandson.

Seth hopped off the swing. "I'm not tired, Grandma."

"Your father used to say the same thing, but once his head rested on the pillow, he'd fall fast asleep. I understand you have more garden planting tomorrow, so you better go to sleep soon." Clara patted Seth's head.

Joshua picked his daughter up. She weighed less than a sack of potatoes. "Grandma is right, Seth. Planting a garden is important work. You'll want to be ready when the sun comes up." Joshua followed everyone through the front door and up the stairs.

It'd been a good day. Good days were something Joshua had learned to appreciate. He'd had more hard days than good after Sarah died. He'd made himself get out of bed when all he wanted to do was sleep. The pain never ceased. He kept going for his kids but it hadn't been easy.

Praying helped, but God still felt far away. Perhaps God had given up on him or was punishing him. He still didn't understand why God didn't heal Sara. They needed her. She left him with a baby and two children they'd taken in from the orphan train. He loved Seth and Rebecca, but after Sara's death, he wanted to send them back to the orphanage. He didn't know how he'd care for three children, the ranch, and his shattered heart.

His pastor had reminded Joshua of the promise he'd made to Sara. He said he would keep their children together. He couldn't have done that without Lizzy. And now he knew he could never repay her for her help.

Joshua laid Rebecca in her bed and kissed her good night. And then he did the same for Emily who slept soundly. *What perfect angels God entrusted me to take care of.* He went to Seth's room, and they prayed. He would pray with the girls in the morning.

Joshua was thankful he'd listened to his pastor and fulfilled his promise. He couldn't imagine his life without the children. They were the biggest reasons he kept going.

~

Lizzy and Mark got married at the First Baptist

Church in Nacogdoches. They'd decorated the white chapel in pink and white azaleas. They picked the flowers from around the church. They thrived there in the filtered light of the dense pine trees. The wedding was in the morning, so they wouldn't have to worry about the humidity getting unbearable in the afternoon. Lizzy wore her grandmother's dress with a few alterations and beads added.

"What a beautiful wedding." Clara hugged Lizzy and wiped away the tears of happiness on her cheeks.

Lizzy's eyes sparkled with unshed tears. "I'm thankful I won't be too far from you and my big brother. I'll need lots of advice on being a good wife."

After the ceremony, women set up tables and chairs for the reception. Clara and Lizzy had been preparing food for two days. Joshua smelled fried chicken, and his stomach rumbled in expectation. They'd have all the fixin's today. His mother's potato salad was the best. A woman from church made the wedding cake.

Partly cloudy skies and the shade of the trees helped keep the temperature low. He enjoyed the fragrance of pine. A small lake sparkled from the sun's rays dancing off the top of the water. Kids begged their mothers to go swimming but none had a change of clothes.

A woman and two young girls walked beside the lake. It was the woman Joshua had attempted to save from falling at the train depot. He had a bruise or two from their encounter. They were leaving. If he'd seen them earlier, he would've said hello.

"Papa," Rebecca pulled on Joshua's hand. "They're done praying. Let's eat."

Joshua had been so busy thinking about the pretty lady he'd missed the prayer. His mother ushered Emily and Seth past a table heaped with food.

He squeezed Rebecca's hand.

"I want a chicken leg before they're gone." Joshua lifted her up, and they walked to the food tables.

Chapter Three

Anna hated waking the girls early. Yesterday had been a good day, but now the reality of taking Laura to her new home weighed heavy on her heart. She was happy Laura had found a family, but Anna's heart broke for Ella. She would be returning to the orphanage with Anna in all probability.

Pastor and Mrs. Smith, Laura's new parents, had been the only ones to attend the orphan train meeting. Anna believed they would be good for Laura. They couldn't have children of their own, and they fell in love with Laura immediately. They'd considered taking Ella too but didn't think they were ready for two children, and they'd wanted a younger child. Laura and Ella depended on each other like sisters. Anna hated separating them. The possibility of finding another set of parents well qualified for Ella wasn't good. All that comforted her was the possibility of keeping Ella herself.

Laura yawned and blinked against the bright morning sun. She sat up when she saw Anna sitting on the bed. "Miss Wilson, why are you crying?"

Anna wiped tears from her cheeks. "Oh dear, I didn't realize I was. I've been thinking how happy I am you've found a family who will love you. Ella and I will miss you." She affected what she hoped was a sincere smile. "This isn't a day to cry, however. Let's have some fun and get you settled with your new family."

"I'll miss you and Ella too. I wish you could both stay in Nacogdoches." Tears flowed from Laura's eyes as she got up and hugged Anna.

"I do too." Anna patted the bed next to her. Laura sat down. "Ella and I will be here for at least two more weeks. I need to check on the families who took in children from previous orphan trains. We'll come visit you as much as we can."

Ella turned over in her bed and looked at Anna and Laura. Her hair was disheveled by sleep. "What are you talking about?"

"I'm reassuring Laura we'll visit her as often as we can in the weeks we're here in Nacogdoches." Anna stood. "Let's get dressed and have breakfast. How do pancakes and eggs sound? We'll go back to the lake and feed the ducks some bread crumbs. We aren't expected at the Smith's until this afternoon."

Laura, always ready for the next adventure, reached for her dress from the chair back. "Pancakes. Yum! I want to feed the ducks. They need breakfast too. I wish we had time for ice cream."

"We'll make time for ice cream." Anna hugged both girls. "I'm proud of you both. You are well-behaved young ladies."

~

Anna grabbed Ella's hand and helped pull her into the buggy. She flipped the reins, and the horses trotted down the road. They were on their way to visit a family who had taken children in from the last orphan train. Anna tried to get Pastor Smith and his wife to keep Ella so she would have time with Laura. The Smiths couldn't because they'd received a telegram the day before saying his Mother wasn't doing well so they left to be with her. "I'm sorry Ella, but it'll just be the two of us today."

"I'm glad I can go. It'll be fun." Ella scooted closer to Anna on the padded bench. "Why can't we stay together, Miss Wilson?"

Anna knew Ella didn't want to go back to the orphanage. "I'm trying to find a way. I want us to always be together. For today though, let's enjoy this adventure. The sun is shining and there's only a couple of clouds dotting the bright blue sky. We're going to a cattle ranch and we should see lots of animals." Anna put her arm around Ella and pulled her close. "Maybe they'll ask us to stay for dinner. A big juicy steak sounds delicious."

Thinking about food made Anna's mouth water and her stomach rumble. It had been a few hours since they'd ate breakfast. They should've bought a couple of sandwiches before they left since the ranch was five miles from town and would take over an hour to get there.

"Ella, if you could have anything you wanted for dinner, what would it be?" Anna asked.

"I love mashed potatoes and brown gravy." Ella smiled at Anna. "And homemade bread warm from the oven. Oh, and apple pie for dessert. Apple pie is my favorite. I'd love to have a yard with lots of apple trees."

"That would be wonderful. We could make pies every day." Anna wondered if Ella's chatter was to cover up her nervousness at meeting new people. They passed a lake and the crystal clear water beckoned Anna. She loved to fish. Her dad taught her when she was four. She should take Ella fishing.

Anna's thoughts returned to her purpose for today. She hoped this visit went well. Most of the time the children were treated well. She often thought the parents could be more loving but at least they provided a safe environment for them. It was when the children were being abused that Anna wished she had another job. She didn't understand how anyone could hurt a child. Enough sad thoughts she wanted to enjoy this time with Ella

~

They turned onto a side road where a big wooden gate stood open. Above the gate they'd hung the letter B. They stopped the horses in front of a two-story white farmhouse. A covered porch ran the full length of the house. Anna hopped down. This had to be the right place, according to the directions the man at the livery had given her, but the place looked deserted. She tied the reins to the hitching post.

Ella got down from the buggy and headed up the porch steps behind Anna. "This house sure is nice. I love the porch swing."

Anna removed her bonnet so she could enjoy the cool breeze. The ride to the ranch left her feeling hot and sweaty. She knocked on the front door. She heard a child crying inside.

A gray-haired woman with her hair flying loose in every direction answered the door. "Hello, can I help you?"

"Hello, my name is Anna Wilson, I'm an agent from the Children's Aid Society in New York City. They require me to visit families who took in children from previous orphan trains. Are you Mrs. Brown?" Anna watched as all the color drained from the woman's face.

"I'm Clara Brown but not the Mrs. Brown you're looking for. I'm the Grandmother of the children you've come to see. Please come in. You look absolutely parched." Clara beckoned Anna and Ella to follow her inside. Clara almost tripped over the wooden toy blocks on the floor behind her. She scooted them off to the side with her foot. "Have a seat. I'll put the kettle on."

Anna and Ella sat in the dining room while Clara went to the kitchen. The table was covered with clothes and toys. Toys were scattered across the floor, and she heard the child crying again from upstairs. Anna wondered if Mrs. Brown was the only one home. "Would you like help?" Anna yelled. "I'd be happy to watch the kettle for you. I hear someone crying."

Clara came back into the dining room with three cups and a bowl of sugar. "I'm sorry everything is such a mess. My daughter had been taking care of the house and my three grandchildren for her brother, but she was married last Saturday. Filling her shoes is harder than I thought. When I was younger, I had six children and this farmhouse to run, but age makes a difference. Let me get Emily up from her nap, and then I'll check on

Rebecca and be back down. Seth is helping in the garden. The water should be hot by then and we'll have tea."

Anna and Ella went into the kitchen to watch the kettle. They sat down at a small table. A young boy ran in through the back door.

"Grandma, I cut my finger."

Anna stood up. "Your grandma went upstairs to check on the girls. Let me see it."

"Who are you?" Seth held up his bloody finger while drops splattered on the floor.

Anna introduced herself and Ella. She grabbed a towel from the kitchen counter and applied pressure to the cut. "How did you cut your finger?"

"I was helping Jake plant the garden, and I tried to cut open a bag with his knife." Tears streamed down Seth's cheeks.

The water in the kettle boiled over. Anna asked Ella to help Seth while she took the kettle off the stove. Clara came into the kitchen holding a brown-haired little girl as a blonde-haired girl followed. She said the youngest girl was Emily, and the oldest was Rebecca.

Clara wasn't surprised by Seth's wound. He must be a rambunctious boy who'd already had his share of accidents. Clara couldn't decide if it needed stitches. She excused herself to go out to the barn and ask Luke's opinion on what to do.

Clara walked into the dining room with a man around Anna's age. She introduced Luke, Mr. Brown's right-hand man, to Anna and Ella.

Anna watched the blonde-haired, blue eyed cowboy examine the cut. The bleeding had stopped.

Luke tussled Seth's hair. "It'll be fine if we clean it

out and bandage it. I better get back to the barn. There's a new calf wanting to make its way into the world."

Clara patted Luke on the shoulder and handed Emily to Anna. She took Seth by the arm. "If you can bear with me a few more minutes, I will have Seth's finger bandaged and I'll be back with some bread and the butter I churned yesterday morning."

Anna grabbed a toy sitting on the table and gave it to Emily. "Clara, please, I need to speak to Mr. and Mrs. Brown. I'm confused by the presence of a toddler. Is Emily their daughter? In the report I have, it says the Browns couldn't have children. That's why they took in Seth and Rebecca. Am I right?"

Clara slumped into a chair. "My daughter-in-law, Sarah, who you call Mrs. Brown, hadn't been able to get pregnant. A couple of months after they took in Seth and Rebecca, they had a miracle. But Sarah died two years ago after giving birth to Emily."

"My son took her passing hard, but he's a great father. His sister, Lizzy, came to keep things going. This cattle ranch demands a lot, but he tries to make it home in time for supper and to play with the children. He loves his children, Miss Wilson."

"I'm sorry. No one told me. I can't imagine how difficult it's been. Ella would love to help you get everything together in the kitchen, wouldn't you?" Anna gave her a wink.

Ella smiled her brightest smile. "Yes, I would."

~

Clara invited Anna and Ella to stay for dinner. They spent the afternoon taking care of the children, picking up the house and helping cook. Anna saw that the house, and the children were too much for Clara to do alone. Mr. Brown needed to find help for Clara or she'd have to find Seth and Rebecca another family.

Clara shooed Anna out of the kitchen and told her to enjoy the porch swing while she set the table. The breeze cooled her off from the work of scrubbing the kitchen floor. She noticed someone had gotten water for the horses. Anna hoped Mr. Brown arrived home soon. They needed to get the horses and buggy back to the livery in Nacogdoches. The climbing roses growing around the porch gave off a sweet smell, and for the first time that day, peace found its way into her soul. If only she could skip the confrontation with Mr. Brown.

Anna's thoughts drifted to Bennett North and his two children, even though those memories were eight years old. In that time, she had gone from living in the home of one of the wealthiest men in New York to traveling the country on an orphan train. Bennett hadn't treated her much better than the orphan children who found themselves with unkind parents. He'd hired her as a nanny when she was seventeen. He treated her as an employee for four years.

That all changed one night when Bennett came into the library while she was reading. He asked her if she could find a good book for him to read. While she looked for it he came up behind her and when she turned around he kissed her. Anna ran to her room. She hoped that the alcohol stole the memories of that evening from his head.

It didn't. After that, he brought her special gifts each day---candy, flowers, and small pieces of jewelry. He told her he cared about her. Anna let her guard down little by little and dreamed of being his wife and mother to the children. Anna thought she was in love with Bennett. His advances increased and her resolve grew weaker until one night she gave in to him.

Two days later he told her to pack her bags and leave. Bennett had proposed to an heiress, and the woman had agreed to marry him. There was no room for Anna in such a life. The morning Anna left, his children stood at the window crying. Her heart broke so many times that day.

Anna had feared she was pregnant, and she didn't have anywhere to go. She walked by the Children's Aid Society where a help wanted sign was posted. Anna got the job cleaning the orphanage for room and board and a small wage. She was relieved when she found out she wasn't pregnant. She felt compassion toward the mothers who left their babies at the orphanage because she understood how fast life changed. Dropping their children off at the orphanage was a plea for a better future for their children.

She worked hard at the orphanage to become an agent. She was one of the few agents who thought the children were more than a job. She fought for them and wanted each one to have a good life.

All of that remembering wearied Anna. She laid her head back and closed her eyes. What was taking Mr. Brown so long? Clara said he got home in time for dinner and to play with the kids, but it didn't look that way to her. He'd barely have time to shovel down his food, pat the children on the heads and tuck them in bed. They needed and deserved more. And why hadn't he noticed his mother needed help? Did he believe the ranch was worth more than three precious children?

Chapter Four

Joshua rode into the yard with his men and spotted two horses and a buggy tied to the hitching post in front of the house. An older girl was playing with his daughters by the flowers. She looked familiar. He rode into the barn and let Luke put his horse, Midnight, up for the night. Joshua was late tonight, and he wanted to spend some time with his children before they went to bed. They'd driven the cattle to better pasture, and it'd taken longer than expected.

How had his Mother done today with the children? He'd helped her with dishes the night before and with getting the children to bed, but they'd both fallen asleep before picking up the house. He missed Lizzy. His Mother was trying, but he worried he was asking too much of her. But what else could he do? He had posted an ad at the post office for a housecleaner and cook so his Mother could concentrate on the children, but no one had responded.

"Father! Seth cut his finger." Rebecca ran into Joshua's arms.

"Is Seth okay?" Joshua asked.

"Yes, Grandma bandaged it." Rebecca made a silly face.

Emily tugged on Joshua's leg, and he hefted the girl into his arms.

Ella watched Joshua interact with the two girls with wide eyes. "Who's your friend?" Joshua asked.

"Are you Mr. Brown?" A young woman concealed by the roses stood up from the porch swing. She was the woman who fell on him at the train depot. He looked back to Ella. He now understood why the girl looked familiar.

"Oh my, you're the man who tried to catch me. You said your name was Joshua, but you never told me your last name." Her face turned a cute shade of pink.

"Aww, yes, Miss Wilson. Right? When I saw your daughter playing with my girls, I thought she looked familiar." Joshua smiled at Anna. "What do we owe the pleasure of this visit to?"

"I'm an agent with the Children's Aid Society from New York City, the orphanage which placed Rebecca and Seth with you and your wife. Ella isn't my daughter, and neither was Laura. They're orphans. Laura is living with Pastor Smith and his wife in town." Anna stepped to the porch's railing and whispered. "Could I talk with you away from the girls?" She sent Ella and the two Brown girls to find Seth.

After the children rounded the corner of the house, Joshua took his cowboy hat off and wiped the dust from his forehead. "I'm afraid you have me at a disadvantage. I didn't know there would be visits from the orphanage. Will you be staying for dinner? I'd like to clean up and see how my son's doing. Can we talk then? It's been a long day."

"We can talk after dinner, as long as it doesn't get too late. We need to head back to town. I'll see if Clara needs help getting dinner on the table." Anna opened the screen door.

Joshua stepped around her and opened the door. He told Miss Wilson that Pastor Smith was their pastor. They had been going to his church for the last five years since him and his wife moved to Nacogdoches. Joshua was certain Laura would have a great family to live with. Pastor Smith and his wife knew how to show love to everyone. They genuinely cared. He couldn't remember ever hearing a sermon from him and not learning something insightful.

Why hadn't the previous agent told them they would be checking on the children periodically? He didn't have anything to hide but it would have been nice to know. The other agent had given them Seth and Rebecca with hardly a word said. The agent acted like he just wanted to be rid of them. He wondered if Miss Wilson was here to ask him to take in Ella since she hadn't been able to find anyone for her. She could be a big help to his mother and the girls. But what was he thinking? He already had three children.

Seth was sitting on the sofa playing with his wooden animals. Joshua sat next to him and asked how his finger was doing. Seth sat the animals down and showed him the wrapped finger. He told Joshua he'd cut it using a knife to open a bag of seeds. Joshua reminded Seth he needed more practice before he could use a knife by himself. Clara yelled dinner was about ready.

"I'm going to wash up." Joshua hugged his son. "I

love you."

Seth snuggled into Joshua's embrace. "I love you too, Father."

~

Joshua leaned back in the rocking chair on the front porch. He wondered what Miss Wilson wanted to talk about. If his mother's conversation at dinner was any indication, it didn't sound like things went well today. His gut told him he would not like what she said. He saw that Ella and Miss Wilson were very close. She wouldn't choose to leave her with a family.

The day weighed heavily on him. He rested his head on the back of the rocker and closed his eyes. They'd had to drive the cattle much farther than he'd expected to find enough grass and fresh water. With more ranchers moving into the area the water was always in short supply by the end of summer.

Miss Wilson was lovely to look at and watching her play with Emily had warmed his heart. The child had loved the attention. Why was he thinking about Miss Wilson, he wasn't interested in complicating his life? All he wanted was to play with his children and go to bed.

The screen door opened.

"I'm sorry I kept you waiting, but I wanted to help your mother clean the kitchen." Anna sat opposite Joshua in the porch swing.

"What do you want to discuss with me, Miss Wilson." Joshua yawned. "It's been a very long day."

"I think everyone's tired and overwhelmed, Mr. Brown. When I got here today, the household was rather chaotic." Anna pushed the swing with her foot.

Joshua leaned forward with his elbows on his knees.

"Some days are that way. The ranch is a busy place. We all have lots to do." A bubble of anger burned in his gut. Was this woman going to blame him for everything that took place today?

Anna sat back in the swing. "I understand things are busy but I don't feel your mother can keep up with it. It would be hard for a younger woman. From what your mother said, Lizzy had a woman who helped three days a week with the cleaning and laundry. Your Mother is fifty-seven and taking care of three young children and a big house. It's too much."

Joshua's heart beat faster. This woman may be an agent with the Children's Aid Society, but this was his family. How could she judge what went on here by one afternoon? He didn't like her attitude. "My mother took care of this house and raised six children. She's more than capable of taking care of three."

"That was a lot of years ago, and she had a housekeeper and cook. She is trying her best, but it's too much. Some things need to change, or I'll find Seth and Rebecca another family to live with." Anna stopped swinging and leaned forward, eye to eye with Joshua. "I won't leave children in a home where their needs aren't being met. I know you aren't intentionally neglecting them, nor is your mother, but not being able to keep up with them can be unintentional neglect."

Joshua stared right back at Anna and raised his voice. "Whoa... you are out of line. My children have never been neglected, and you aren't taking them anywhere!" Evidently, his mother and Anna had had quite an extensive talk today. He wished it hadn't been so informative.

Anna raised her voice. "I will remove the children,

Mr. Brown, if you can't find help for your mother. If I make the sheriff aware of the situation, he will act on my word." She walked over to the porch railing. "A woman your mother's age can't be expected to keep up with all of this."

"I assume, Miss Wilson, you don't have children of your own. If you did you would understand love is the most important thing a child needs. I love all three of my children. The rest we will take care of without your interference." Joshua stood toe to toe with Anna. "I promised my dying wife I would keep our children together, and I will do just that, Miss Wilson. You're not taking them anywhere." Joshua felt the tension mounting. His heart was pounding. Why was this woman threatening to tear his home apart over a messy house and a cut finger? He wanted to pick her up, set her on the buggy seat and send her back to town.

Anna stood her ground. "You're right, I don't have children, but I've been taking care of children since I was seventeen. You're blind to her not being able to do this alone. I understand your attachment to Seth and Rebecca and the promise you made to your wife. She would want her children well cared for, even if it meant them leaving your home. They're young and I believe many families would take them in."

"My children will not leave this ranch and I have more than an attachment to them. I've posted an ad for a housecleaner and cook at the post office. I expect a response any day." Joshua looked intently into Anna's eyes. He'd never seen eyes more bright and beautiful. But just how in the world could he be thinking such a thing as she was threatening to take his children away? The woman was infuriating.

"Legally, I hope you understand, Seth and Rebecca are not your children. They were placed in your care. And I'm here to help. I want this situation to work for everyone's sake. We'll work together to find a solution. Where is the woman who helped Lizzy? Are there family members who could help? Is there anyone in your church?"

This woman was unrelenting. He had to come up with an idea which would satisfy her, but what? "Lizzy's housekeeper followed her to her new home. My brothers and their wives are raising children of their own. I asked my pastor if he knew anyone. He didn't." Joshua couldn't think while looking into Anna's face. Instead, he watched his men feed the livestock in the corrals. They had to wonder what was taking place. They glanced over every few minutes. How had this day gone downhill so fast? A shooting star streaked across the sky. It had gotten late, and he didn't see how Miss Wilson would make it back to town tonight.

Anna looked to the growing darkness and frowned. "It's too late to solve your problems tonight. I'll get Ella and leave. We will come tomorrow to help your mother. At some point, though, I must make other arrangements for the children."

The children had given him a reason to wake up each day after Sarah's death. He couldn't lose them too. A crazy thought popped into Joshua's head. And before he thought about it, he blurted it out. "I have a proposition for you, Miss Wilson. Would you stay in the house and help my mother until I can find someone else? I'll pay you and give you room and board."

Anna's brow creased with worry.

"I'll move into the bunkhouse. In fact, there's no

reason for you to go back to Nacogdoches. Why don't you stay here tonight? I couldn't allow you to take the chance of heading back in the dark. I'll send one of my men with you tomorrow to get your bags and return the horses and buggy to the livery. I'll even pay the extra day's rental." Joshua studied Anna's face, hoping she didn't think his offer was too crazy to accept.

"Mr. Brown, your proposal simply won't work. I'm under the employment of the Children's Aid Society. I have to visit other families before I can return to New York City." Anna turned on her heel to collect Ella from the house.

Anna paused inside the house to collect her thoughts. Was the man crazy? She couldn't neglect her responsibilities for one family. Besides, she was expected back in New York City.

A male voice interrupted her thoughts. "Hey boss, do you need us to do something with these horses tonight? They've been tied up for a few hours and I'm sure they're hungry."

"Yes, feed and stable the horses for the night. I'll be sleeping in the bunkhouse."

Luke clicked his tongue, and the horses followed him toward the barn.

Joshua heard a gasp from just inside the door. Anna stepped into the waning light. There was no mistaking the shock on her face. "I didn't agree to this, Mr. Brown. You can't force me to do something because it solves your problems." Anna descended the stairs and called after Joshua's man, who didn't even acknowledge her. "I'm getting Ella and please have your man bring the horses back."

"Miss Wilson, staying here is your safest option.

You have the night to consider accepting my job offer. I hope you'll see that my plan has benefits for both of us. There's no reason why you can't keep up with your visits. Ella can stay here with my mother while you're gone. My horse and buggy are yours to command. One of my men can go along to assure your safety." Joshua gestured toward the door.

"All right, we'll stay tonight, and I'll think on your offer, but I won't make any promises." Anna let the screen door slam behind her.

Joshua stared at the door. This could be the worst idea he'd ever had. He just couldn't let Miss Wilson take Seth and Rebecca. Joshua's stomach clenched at the thought of losing his children. He had fixed the problem temporarily, but he had no idea what the permanent solution would be. Most women in the west were married with their own families or not the type he wanted around his children.

I hope you have an answer God because I sure don't.

Trust me, Joshua.

Joshua looked around to see who had said that. Only earth and sky filled the night. He must be more tired than he thought.

Chapter Five

The porch was Anna's one refuge on the ranch in the two weeks she had been with the Brown family. She pushed the swing into a lazy rhythm to quiet herself from the day's busyness. Thousands of stars dotted the blue expanse of the Texan sky. This was where the family gathered each evening after dinner, and although she would never admit it to Joshua, Anna had enjoyed being part of their family.

The children pushed each other on a swing hanging from an ancient oak. Anna relished the joy apparent in Ella as she played with the Brown children. When the time came, leaving would be difficult for Ella, and for her.

"Anna, I appreciate your help. It's a blessing God brought you and Ella here when He did. I still can't believe I broke my arm. My goodness, I've walked up and down those stairs a million times." Clara rubbed the injured arm, and Anna wondered if she needed some willow bark tea.

"Joshua would've had to stay at the house if you

41

hadn't been here, which would've left the ranch without a boss. I've told him he should hire a foreman, but he hasn't yet." Clara looked at her son and winked.

"I do need to hire a foreman, but am torn between two men. Jim's been here two years and is great working the cattle. Luke's been here three years and takes care of the horses and buildings. I never worry about either of them doing what needs done. I've gotten to know the men better since I've been staying in the bunkhouse. I see how they act when I'm not usually watching. Both Jim and Luke are level-headed and reliable." Joshua took a drink of his tea.

"Maybe you need two foremen. This is a big ranch. There's plenty of work to go around." Clara passed a plate of cookies to Joshua.

Anna leaned back against the swing and closed her eyes. If she wished hard enough, could she bring her parents back? She would love to talk with them as Clara and Joshua were doing. Anna had talked with her parents about everything. She remembered being six and arguing with her best friend. Her best friend punched her in the face and gave Anna a bloody nose. Anna got mad and never wanted to be friends with her again. When she talked to her mother about it, she said she needed to forgive her friend and apologize for what she had said. Anna didn't want to apologize, but she did and so did her friend and they were soon best friends again.

Clara switched topics. She wanted to try a new variety of corn, Silver Queen, she had read about it in the seed catalog.

Sweet corn was the best, it was hard to believe it was a vegetable. Anna loved when the plants first popped up through the dirt, rewarding her for all the digging and planting each spring. Gardening with her mother had been one of Anna's favorite things. They planted vegetables, herbs, and flowers. They had apple and pear trees too. Anna and her mother kept up with the weeding so they wouldn't choke the plants out. They'd grown every vegetable they ate in the summer.

"I love sitting under these roses. It reminds me of home." Anna blinked away unshed tears.

Clara patted Anna's hand. "Did your mother grow roses?"

"She did."

"It's hard when we lose the people we love the most. We feel cheated out of time with them. When my husband, William, died, I felt that way. Life doesn't prepare us for loss or grief. It throws us into sorrow and expects us to find a way through. I'm thankful God was there for me."

Anna didn't know why Clara was saying God was there for her. How could He be there for her and let her husband die? Anna didn't understand how people gave God a pass on letting bad things happen. If He was so loving and good then why did He allow so much heartbreak?

"God wasn't with me when my parents died. A loving God wouldn't take my parents when they were all I had or leave you without your husband. He wouldn't take Joshua's wife from him or her newborn baby. Would a loving God leave so many children on the streets of New York City without their parents? The living conditions are so bad they die from disease.

"I haven't felt close to God since I was a little girl and I wonder if I made even that up in my head." Anna closed her eyes. She refused to cry. "I've lived without God for over ten years. I don't need Him. He changes nothing."

Anna looked from Clara to Joshua and checked to see that the children hadn't heard her. "I'm sorry. I shouldn't have said all that. God is real to both of you. The minister who started the Children's Aid Society would not agree with me and would dismiss me if he heard what I said. I don't tell the children my opinions because they are comforted by the idea God is watching over them." Anna watched the children pushing each other on the swing.

"We won't tell anyone, Anna. I'm sorry you feel betrayed by God. When William died I was upset at God for a time. I don't know why He didn't heal William, or Sarah, or your parents, but He loves us." Clara looked at Joshua. "Were you mad at God when you lost Sarah?"

"At times, but those feelings didn't bring me peace. I wanted to die with Sarah as I held her hand and looked into her eyes as she took her last breath. A part of me did. After two years, the pain is less but I still miss her. When I look at Emily, I see Sarah and know God left me a part of her. I want Sarah to be proud." Joshua bent his head.

Clara rubbed his back. "I love you, son. Sarah would be proud of how you've kept your family together." Clara looked at Anna. "Your parents would be proud of your tender heart and how you fight for the rights of children who have no one. Even though you say God doesn't love us because of the things He allows in our life, I see His heart for all His children in you. We can know He loves us because He was willing to give His life for those who love Him and those who don't. I'm sorry I made everyone sad. I didn't mean to. Why don't we play a game with the kids before bed? We need happy thoughts and feelings so we can sleep well."

Joshua stood up. "Sounds good. I'm ready to beat y'all." He yelled at the kids. "Let's play a game. Grandma might even have more cookies."

Anna got up as the kids ran into the house. *Could God still love her?* She found it hard to believe.

~

Anna waited for Luke to finish harnessing the horses. She hoped all the extra preparations they'd done yesterday would get the family through the afternoon without her. She couldn't neglect her responsibilities to the orphans and their families any longer. She had telegraphed the Children's Aid Society to let them know she would be in Texas for a lot longer than originally planned.

"Your buggy's ready, Ma'am." Luke tied the horses to the hitching rail. "Are you?"

"I am. I'm visiting the Weaver farm." Anna grabbed the buggy bench so she could pull herself up.

"Let me help you." Luke lifted her into the buggy. "Be careful, some of the things I've heard about Henry Weaver aren't good. If you're not back in three hours, I'll head that way. Better yet, I can send one of the men with you, if you want." Luke winked at her.

Anna's face and neck got warm. "I'm sure I'll be fine, but thank you, Mr. Nelson. I've had to go by myself in the other towns. I'm used to relating to all types of people."

"It's just, Luke, Ma'am." He handed the reins to

her. "Do you know where you're headed?"

"Yes, Mr. Brown, drew a map for me last night." Anna tucked her skirt around her legs.

Luke smiled. "Good. See you when you get back." His cowboy charm knew no end.

Anna turned the horses and headed west. *Did Luke just flirt with me*? She couldn't remember the last time a man winked at her. It felt nice. Most men considered her too old for marriage. They wanted a younger woman who'd have a better chance of producing children.

Joshua had voiced concern about her going to the Weaver farm alone too. Anna told him she'd be fine. Although, to be honest, visiting new families made her anxious. There was no way to know what waited for her at someone else's home.

Anna loved the big Texas sky, but the humidity was hard to get used to. Sweat ran down her back, and she wiped her forehead multiple times with her hankie. She understood why the men wore bandanas.

The road to the Weaver farm seemed endless, but Joshua said it would only take an hour to get there. With the road open before her, Anna realized she really didn't want to travel anymore. She'd seen many children gain a chance at a better life, but some children ended up in worse situations. In all the hours she'd spent on trains and dusty wagons, Anna had wondered how to make the situation better for all children. It came down to weeding out the unsuitable families before placing a child in their home. Children should only go with families approved by the sheriff and respected leaders of their community. They needed someone local to check on them. Waiting two or three years for an agent to follow up was too long. And the children needed a temporary place to stay if there were problems with a family. All of that meant that the children needed to be more of a priority.

~

Anna urged the horses down a rutted track. A rundown house and barn stood in the distance. The buildings looked as if the slightest breeze would blow them over. She didn't see anyone, so she went around the house. A woman not much older than Anna bent over the garden, pulling weeds. The hem of her dress was ragged and dirty. The garden was sparse. Everything wilted in the summer heat. Clothes hung on a rope tied between two trees. Anna wondered how the woman had managed to wring the water out of them without shredding the cloth.

Anna's parents never had extra money, but they were rich compared to how this family lived. Anna feared she might throw up. She knew this feeling well. Whenever a family situation was so bad she knew she'd have to take the children out of the home, it made her sick.

"Hello." Anna yelled as she pulled back on the reins. "Are you Mrs. Weaver?"

"I am. Who are you? We don't like strangers here." The woman straightened and walked toward Anna.

"I'm Miss Wilson, an agent for the Children's Aid Society. I'm checking up on Noah and Jack Stanton to see how they're doing. I came into town a couple of weeks ago with an orphan train. My job is to find families for the new orphans and to check on the children from previous orphan trains." Anna went to get down from the buggy.

"No need to get off your buggy." The woman glanced toward the woods behind her. "They ain't here. They're hunting with my husband. The boys are fine, no need to come back."

Anna sat down. "I will be back. It's my responsibility to visit with the children. When can I do that?"

"We're busy every day. Sundays the boys work in the barn so it might be your best chance." Mrs. Weaver looked around again.

"The children shouldn't be working every day. Do they have time to play and read? Are they in school? They must attend school. That is a stipulation of them staying with you." Anna watched Mrs. Weaver nervously glance around. *Was she afraid?*

"Idle hands lead to trouble. We're teaching them hard work, ain't nothing wrong with that." Mrs. Weaver brushed mud from her dress.

Anna picked up the reins. "The boys need to be in school, not working all day. It is a requirement if you care for an orphan from the Children's Aid Society that they attend classes until they are fourteen. I'll take them out of your home and find a family who will make sure they're in school, if you won't."

Mrs. Weaver's face went bright red. "I think you better leave. Those boys ain't going nowhere. They belong to me and my husband. We give them food, a house and clothes. They don't need nothin' else." Mrs. Weaver turned her back on Anna and walked to the garden.

"I'll be back Sunday afternoon." Anna yelled. "Children need more than food, clothes and a home. They need love, Mrs. Weaver. I expect both boys, and you, and your husband to be here when I arrive." Anna swatted the reins and urged the horses to get moving.

What a hateful woman.

Anna had a bad feeling about Mr. and Mrs. Weaver. The woman had talked about the boys as if they were slaves. She considered whether or not she should talk with the sheriff, but she only had suspicions. She could make her visit as she promised on Sunday. If Jack and Noah were being mistreated, she'd take the boys and go to the sheriff. Or she might have to ask Mr. Brown if the boys could stay at the ranch temporarily.

She regretted continuing on when the other agent had fallen ill and had to be hospitalized. There seemed no reason to delay the trip, and especially to delay finding families for the children on the train. She realized now that she should have stayed in Troy, Missouri until another agent could take his place. Having someone to share in the responsibility of a difficult family like the Weavers now seemed the wisest choice. Anna had a history of responding before thinking of the consequences. It could be why she found herself in difficult situations just like this. In spite of her shortsightedness, she hoped Jack and Noah would be safe until she got back to the Weavers.

Chapter Six

Thunder woke Joshua from a restless night of tossing and turning. His mind never shut down, even in sleep. His dreams of what used to be left him disappointed when he woke. He slept in a small room apart from the other men in the bunkhouse, but he heard every snore. He worried Miss Wilson would take Seth and Rebecca if he couldn't find help for his mother. No one had answered his ad for a housekeeper and cook.

Rain pounded the roof. The weather wouldn't let them get much work done today. He'd been working a lot. A rainy day gave him a chance to spend time with his children. It also gave him time to consider hard choices that could be in his future. For one, maybe he had bitten off more than he could chew with a ranch this size. Now that the children depended only on him, he had to consider how his long days affected them. It might be time to sell the ranch. If the ranch came between keeping his children and the ranch, he'd sell it. He didn't have experience at anything other than ranching, but he could learn.

The smell of rain washed over him and brought back memories of when Sarah and he were courting. He had taken her fishing at Pine Lake. They didn't notice the clouds covering the sky until the wind blew his hat off. That got their attention. Joshua and Sarah loaded the wagon and headed to her parents' farm. They'd gone halfway when the clouds had opened up and soaked them to their cores. They had laughed often when remembering that day.

Joshua longed to hear Sarah laugh just once more, to hold her in his arms, and see her beautiful smile. Those days would never return. Somehow he had to live without her.

The last two years had been a blur. He made an effort to be there for his children but sometimes the grief overwhelmed him. He went on long walks and prayed just so the pain wouldn't suck him under. The gaping hole in his heart never filled, but God gave him strength to bear it.

Lizzy had helped so much with the children. They all loved her, and it seemed like they could go on forever with her help. His mother tried to fill her shoes, but it was too hard for her to take care of everything. Things were running smoothly since Miss Wilson had been there. She didn't seem to mind that the kids followed her everywhere.

Still, Miss Wilson was a difficult woman to figure out. Clearly, she loved children but why hadn't she married? She'd be a great mother. There weren't many men who wouldn't call her pretty.

She was definitely pretty, but she didn't look anything like Sarah. Sarah had had blonde hair and bright blue eyes. He'd told her they were bluer than the sky. Miss Wilson wore her hair in a bun. It was the color of chocolate toffee and her eyes were hazel. She was on the short side but Sarah had been tall for a woman, which fit Joshua just fine, as he was over six feet.

Why am I comparing Miss Wilson to Sarah? No one can ever measure up to my Sarah.

Joshua sat up and stretched. He had kinks in every muscle in his back from the rock hard mattress. He missed his feather bed in the house. His mother had been right, he should make someone a foreman. He wanted time with his family, a far less drastic move than selling the ranch. If he couldn't find a housekeeper, he'd have to be home more or Miss Wilson would take two of his children. He would not let that happen.

One of his cow hands stuck his head in the door. "Hey boss, are we moving the cattle today? It's raining buckets, and the lightning isn't letting up." Jim pulled his suspenders up.

"Let's wait a few hours and see if it settles down. While we're waiting, the men can clean out this bunkhouse and the other buildings. I'll ask Luke to keep them busy. He knows what needs done. I will spend the day with my children." Joshua stood up, put his pants on, and buttoned up his shirt. "I want to get together with you and Luke today as well."

Rain pelted him the minute he walked outside, so he made a run for it. He was soaked through by the time he reached the back porch. He brushed the water from his hat and took in the stormy gray sky. He decided that the men should stay at the ranch today, lightning or not. He didn't want any of them getting sick.

Joshua smelled bacon and cinnamon. The aroma was heavenly. He took off his muddy boots and left them on the back porch. He hung his jacket and hat inside the door and walked into the warm kitchen. Miss Wilson wore his mother's yellow apron. It reached nearly to her ankles. "Good morning. You're up early, Miss Wilson."

Anna smiled over her shoulder. "Getting a head start before the kids wake up and want their breakfast." She wiped her hands on the apron. "Shouldn't we drop the Miss and Mr. since we're around each other every day? Please call me, Anna."

"Sounds like a good idea." Anna seemed to be in a good mood. Joshua sat at the table. "Sure is raining hard. What are you making that smells so delicious?"

"Apple Pie Cinnamon Rolls. My mother would make these at least once a month for my father and me. They were my favorite. I set the bread to rising last night and added the filling this morning. They should be done in a few minutes. I'm keeping scrambled eggs and bacon warm too. Would you like coffee?" Anna grabbed two mugs off the shelf.

"Coffee sounds great. It's chilly outside." Joshua took a mug from Anna. "Have you spoken to my mother this morning?"

"Not yet." Anna poured Joshua some coffee. "I told her to sleep in, but I'm sure she'll be up any moment."

"The coffee's great." Joshua took another drink.

Joshua watched Anna add cream and sugar to her coffee. She asked if he would be going to the pastures with it raining so hard. Joshua explained they stayed inside during lightning storms unless an emergency came up. He said he'd be going over paperwork and helping Clara and her with the children. "I'm looking forward to a day at home."

Anna had left her hair down, and it went past the middle of her back. It hung in waves. *It's a shame she always has it in a bun. Why should I care? This woman threatened to take my children away.* Joshua couldn't understand why he was distracted by this woman. The children, and ranch were enough to keep him occupied. He refused to go starry-eyed over the first woman he'd been around in two years.

Clara walked into the kitchen and Joshua took that as his exit to get the children. He wanted something to do, so he wouldn't be admiring Anna's hair.

~

Joshua sat in his favorite chair in the living room, watching the fire burn in the hearth before he went out to the bunkhouse. He wasn't anxious to leave the warmth of the house for the chill of the bunkhouse. The men never paid attention to the fire. They were too busy playing cards.

Joshua rubbed his thighs. They ached from crouching at the tea table the girls had created for an afternoon party. The scrape on his knee burned under his jeans. Seth had talked him into a game of tag. Chasing Seth down the hall he'd slipped on a rug. There may have been a good reason his mother always told him not to run in the house. Reading books had given him a chance to recover before helping his mother and Anna with supper. Although the storm still raged outside, he felt a sense of contentment that hadn't been his since Sarah died.

The house was finally quiet. Everyone except Anna had gone to bed. Pots clanged and there was whisking from the kitchen where she was making something for breakfast. He hoped it would be as good as the apple pie rolls this morning. He could've eaten the whole pan himself. A clap of thunder sounded over the house. It would be another restless night.

"I'm finished with what I was doing and thought I'd drink a cup of tea before I go to bed. Can I bring you something?" Anna stood in the doorway to the dining room.

"No thanks. I'm gonna sit here a little longer and then go to the bunkhouse." Joshua watched her hesitate as if she wasn't sure what to do.

Boom! A deafening crash rattled the house. Joshua went over to the window. "I can't make out anything, it's too dark. I'm going outside. It sounded like lightning struck something."

"Let me get my coat and I'll go too." Anna grabbed her jacket off the coat hook by the back door.

Joshua stepped in between Anna and the door. "You might want to stay inside. It's raining and I'm not certain what happened. We do have tornados in Texas but it sounded more like lightning struck close by."

Clara walked into the kitchen, "What was that loud noise?"

"Mother, please try to talk Anna into staying inside." Joshua hurried out the back door.

"Why don't you stay inside in case the children wake up?" Clara asked.

"I'd rather see what went on than be in here worrying." Anna put her coat on and headed out the door.

Joshua ran through the mud with Anna right behind him. A tree laid across the side of the barn. Jim went over to him when they made it inside. He told Joshua the tree looked stable where it was but they had a huge hole to repair in the roof. They would cut the tree up tomorrow so the barn could be repaired. They moved the animals from the damaged side of the barn to different areas. Joshua was glad it wasn't worse, and no one had gotten hurt. Joshua thanked Jim and told him to get some sleep. They'd change their meeting to a different time.

Joshua glanced at Anna. She was shivering from the cold wet rain. "You should go back to the house, it's chilly out here."

Joshua heard a loud whinny from one of the stalls. Luke was standing in front of the stall.

"Luke, what's going on?" Joshua yelled.

"Starlight is in labor." Luke replied.

Starlight was Joshua's favorite mare. Luke said she hadn't even moved when the tree struck the barn. Joshua told Luke he'd watch her as he wouldn't be able to sleep, anyway. Luke laughed and said lightning storms helped him rest as long as they didn't hit any buildings around him.

Anna peeked into the stall. Her eyes went wide at the site of the laboring horse. "Would you care if I stayed and watched Starlight give birth? I've always wanted to see an animal have a baby, especially a horse. I love horses. They're so beautiful."

"It might be five or six hours before she gives birth. It's cold and will get colder. You don't want to get sick." Joshua looked over the stall door at Starlight.

"I don't mind. It will be worth it. I'll grab blankets and coffee from the house and let Clara know what happened, so she can go back to bed." Anna left.

Great.

He'd wanted to be alone. At least the blankets and coffee would be helpful. He unlocked the stall door and went in. Starlight was lying down on a fresh bed of hay. Luke had stacked hay bundles in the corner to sit on. Joshua never failed to notice the extra things Luke and Jim did. They didn't just do their jobs, but they always did more. He was thankful they had chosen his ranch to work at. Joshua ran his hands down Starlight's sides, everything felt good.

The rain pelted the barn roof. They needed rain, but he could do without the lightning. If it ignited a fire, it could put a lot of ranches in danger. He chastised himself for borrowing trouble. Seeing Starlight's foal into the world required his full attention. No matter how many births he'd watched, Joshua never tired of the miracle of life. It was the most rewarding part of having a ranch. He had to agree with Anna, calves were cute but foals were majestic.

"Can you open the door for me, my hands are full?" Anna asked.

"Let me have the blankets." The top one felt damp as Joshua took the pile from Anna. "This won't keep anyone warm."

Anna held two cups of coffee in one hand and water ran down her face. "It's pouring out there, and I couldn't run because I had the coffee."

"You need to get dry clothes on, so you won't catch a chill. Sitting here for a few hours in wet clothes wouldn't be a good idea. If you'd rather stay inside, I understand." Joshua took the cups of coffee and sat them on the hay.

"You're right, but I don't want to miss this. I'll

bring more blankets and hold one over me, so everything will stay dry." Anna closed the stall door behind her.

Joshua was afraid that would be her response. *Oh well, I've lived through worse.* He sat down and sipped one of the cups of coffee. It was hot. *At least she makes great coffee.* Starlight moved around. This wasn't her first foal, so he hoped there wouldn't be any difficulties. He didn't know how Anna would do if there were complications. Joshua laid his head back against the hay. The day had caught up with him.

I can sleep a few minutes before Anna gets back. It will be a long night.

~

Anna shook Joshua's shoulder. "Joshua, something might be wrong. Starlight's been really restless and making strange noises."

Joshua threw the blanket off him, which Anna must have placed over him, and rushed to Starlight.

"Is she all right?" Anna wrapped a blanket tighter around her shoulders.

"I believe so. Her labor is getting stronger so she will be more restless. This is her third foal, so I'm expecting it to go well." Joshua sat on the hay bales. "Guess my coffee's cold. The one sip I had was good. So much for saying I wouldn't be able to sleep. Are you warm?"

"The blankets are nice. I also put on warmer clothes when I went back to the house." Anna laid her head against the hay.

"If you need to sleep, I'll wake you when Starlight's ready." Joshua draped the blanket he'd discarded around his shoulders.

"I'm too excited to sleep. I haven't heard any thunder lately, so maybe the storm's over. I think that's why all the men went to the bunkhouse. Luke said if you need help, to wake him." Anna tried pushing loose curls back into her bun, but the pins kept falling out from the weight of her damp hair. Her hair fell down past her shoulders.

"You talked to Luke?"

Anna struggled to get her hair back into a bun but it wasn't cooperating. "He explained what Starlight might do. He's a great guy. You must be glad to have his help." Anna gave up, her hair stayed down.

"I am. I wouldn't trust very many of my men with watching over the ranch when I'm away." Joshua sighed. He was glad she didn't get her hair back in a bun. With her hair down the years disappeared from her face and she could pass for a young woman barely out of her teen years. *How had he become distracted again?* "How long have you worked for the Children's Aid Society?"

Anna laid another blanket over her lap. "I've been there eight years. This is the second orphan train I've been on, and it will be my last. I'm tired of traveling and want to find a home where Ella and I can live. I'm thinking of getting a teaching certificate."

"What did you do before you went to work there?" Joshua wished his coffee was hot.

"My parents died when I was seventeen. They owed too much on their mortgage, so the bank sold everything at an auction to cover their debts. I didn't have any relatives to stay with, so I found a job as a nanny." Anna paused and looked away from Joshua.

"How did you find that job?" Joshua sat back

against the hay. He wanted to learn more about this woman who traveled the west finding homes for orphans.

"A son of my father's friend had a position available, so I worked for him. I was there four years and then went to the orphanage." Anna wouldn't look at Joshua.

"Why did you leave a nanny position to work at an orphanage? It seems working for a family would be better." Joshua asked.

Anna kept her eyes on the barn rafters. "The father married, so he let me go. It's complicated." She looked at Joshua. There were tears in her eyes. "That's enough about my past. How did you meet Sarah?"

That question was a punch to his gut. He guessed he earned it after questioning her about a past that obviously made her uncomfortable. There was more than what she'd said to Anna's story, he was certain of it. He still found it difficult to talk about Sarah. He warned himself to keep the story simple. "We met at school. I don't remember a time I didn't have a crush on her. We were best friends and then we fell in love." Joshua stopped for a moment. "I can't believe she's gone."

Joshua studied Anna. The tears she'd held in check slid down her cheeks. He touched her face and wiped away a tear with his thumb. He scooted nearer to her. Her pulse throbbed beneath his hand, and for the first time since Sarah died, he desired to kiss another woman. He caressed her hair, the strands felt like silk. She shut her eyes. He brushed his lips across hers and electricity shot through him. She trembled. He should stop but an unseen force drew him nearer. Joshua moved his hand to the back of her neck and his fingers massaged her tense muscles. He kissed her. She wrapped her arms around him. He'd convinced himself all these feelings were buried with Sarah, but now he knew different. She tilted her head back, and they deepened their kiss.

Starlight moaned. Joshua and Anna backed away from each other. "I'm sorry." He managed to say before he got up and checked the horse.

"Looks like we'll have a foal soon." Joshua glanced at Anna. Tears ran down her cheeks once more. He walked over to her and bent down. "I'm sorry, I shouldn't have kissed you. I'm feeling all kinds of emotions, the biggest one being guilt. I'm not ready to let go of Sarah. I'm attracted to you. You're a beautiful woman, but you're also the woman who told me she'd take my children away. You'll be going back to New York City, so I promise I won't kiss you again." Joshua pulled her to her feet and wiped the tears away. "Let's get this foal here. After some sleep, I'm confident we'll go back to being adversaries."

"I've never been your adversary," Sarah whispered. "I only want what's best for the children."

Joshua barely heard her words. *What had he started?*

Chapter Seven

The sun's rays shone down on Anna as she opened her eyes. She rolled over in bed and glanced out the window. The sun was directly above her. *No one woke me.* The log cabin quilt beckoned her to remain underneath its warm shelter. Anna stretched and nestled back into the folds of the quilt.

She'd been so cold when she came in from the barn. Anna hadn't told Joshua because he would have wanted her to go back to the house before the foal was born. Thoughts of being in the barn with him brought heat rushing to cheeks. *Why did I let Joshua kiss me?* Anna didn't know if she could be in the same room with him without blushing. Over the last eight years she'd reconciled herself to never getting involved with another man. She'd thought Joshua despised her because she'd threatened him. The kiss though, was not from a man who despised her. Joshua must be lonely and Anna was too. Loneliness wasn't a basis for a relationship, only trouble. She needed to avoid being alone with him.

Anna needed to speed up checking on the families in Nacogdoches, so she could return to New York City and work on getting her teaching certificate. If she prolonged her time on the ranch, it would only get more complicated and harder for her and Ella to leave. She didn't want to live in a big city anymore.

Knock. Knock.

"Miss Wilson, are you awake?" Ella yelled through the door.

Anna swung her legs out of bed, put on her robe and opened the door.

Ella tucked a red curl behind her ear. "Mr. Brown said to let you sleep because you were up most of the night. He took all of us out to see Starlight's baby before he rode out to check on the cattle early this morning. The foal's so cute!"

Anna smiled. "I would've loved to have gone out to see the foal with you. You should have woke me?"

Ella tugged Anna toward the clothes she'd draped over a chair in haste the night before. "You need to get dressed. Mrs. Brown packed a picnic so we can walk down to the pond and eat lunch. I can't wait. It will just be all us girls and Seth."

~

Clara started down the church steps. "Pastor Smith's sermons are the best."

"His messages always challenge me." Joshua put his hand under Clara's elbow to make sure she made it down the stairs with no mishaps.

Anna followed behind carrying Emily. Seth played tag on the church's lawn with a bunch of boys. Rebecca and her friends took their dolls under the shade of an oak tree. Ella and Laura huddled on a bench with their heads together.

Members of the church congregation had set up tables on the east side of the building. Food occupied every spare inch of the tables. The church had a lunch potluck once a month so everyone could talk and get better acquainted. Anna and Clara had cooked all day Saturday while Ella kept an eye on the children. They'd made a big pot roast with potatoes, carrots and onions, three pans of rolls and two deep dish apple pies.

Luke walked toward them. He cleaned up well. His face was freshly shaven, and he looked handsome in his vest and tie. He took his hat off and ran his fingers through his hair. "Howdy Ma'am. I haven't seen you since that feisty colt arrived. I've been waiting for you to come see him again. Mr. Brown said you could have the honor of naming him because you helped with the birth."

Anna felt her cheeks get warm. *Would she ever stop thinking about Joshua's kiss when someone mentioned that night?* "I'm doing well. Mr. Brown didn't mention he wanted me to name the colt. Now that I know, I'll go see him. I'm sure he's even cuter and, of course, he has to have a name."

"Watching your first birth is a powerful experience." Luke smiled at Anna. "Would you like to take a walk by the lake until they're ready for us to eat?"

Anna consented to walk with Luke and handed Emily to Clara. When she put her hand in the crook of his arm, there weren't any sparks. Next to Joshua, he was the best looking man here. He was kind and protective, but Anna thought of him as a brother. She caught the glares of many women watching her and

Luke. She was confident he wouldn't have a problem finding a girl.

"How do you like Nacogdoches? I'm sure it's a lot different than New York City." Luke walked toward the area where some of the children were feeding ducks.

"It's completely different. I like it. Everyone treats you like family and they support each other." Anna sat on a bench behind the children and Luke sat beside her.

Anna learned that Luke had been in Nacogdoches for three years. His parents lived in Houston, Texas. He wanted to have his own ranch one day. That's why he came here, so he could learn from the best. Joshua had a reputation for having one of the finest cattle ranches in east Texas. Luke had worked for him a year before his wife died. He had enjoyed being around them and watching how they supported each other. He had worried that the grief from losing Sarah would be too much for Joshua, but little by little, Luke saw that he'd gotten back to living.

Anna learned a lot she didn't know as Luke talked with her. He was easy to be with, and Anna relaxed for the first time in days. He wanted to know if she'd ever live anywhere besides New York City, and she told him she was thinking about it. Pastor Smith interrupted their conversation as he asked everybody to gather around the tables. He blessed the food and thanked everyone for coming.

Luke and Anna got in line. Ella and Laura were chatting behind them. Anna noticed a red-haired woman speaking with Joshua in a different line. The woman smiled at nearly every word he said. If someone needed a picture for the definition of enraptured, it could be of the woman gazing at Joshua. Anna wished she would find somebody different to talk to.

"Who's the red-haired woman talking with Mr. Brown?" Anna asked Luke.

"That's our school teacher, Miss Baker. She moved here three years ago and has been doing a great job with the children; at least that's what I've been told." Luke took two plates and gave one to Anna.

Anna filled her plate with chicken, potato salad and a roll. Joshua was serving the lovely Miss Baker. He even carried her plate to the blankets Clara had spread out. Clara was feeding Emily while Seth and Rebecca ate. Anna felt a twinge of guilt because she hadn't helped Clara get the kids plates filled. Anna realized with a start that she was thinking of the children as her family. They'd worked their way into her heart, and it would be tough to leave them when the time came. She didn't enjoy watching another woman look so content with Joshua.

"Do you want to eat with everyone or go back to the lake? I'll carry the plates if you can get the drinks." Luke held his hand out for her plate.

They decided to eat with everyone else and Anna asked Pastor and Mrs. Smith if Laura could join them. Once everyone had their food and places to sit, Anna settled down on the blanket. *This ought to be fun. Miss Baker has Luke on one side and Joshua on the other. I have the children. Oh well, it's how my life has always been.* Miss Baker was telling Luke, how wonderful it was to see him, as it had been too long. Clearly, she and Luke knew each other well. In fact, Anna sensed a relationship which extended beyond friendship.

Although now, Miss Baker was batting her eyes at Joshua. *How many men could one woman flirt with during a potluck?* Luke introduced Anna to Julia Baker. They talked about their shared interest in children. Julia knew Anna was staying at the ranch and was an agent on the orphan trains. She told Anna she wouldn't find a better father than Joshua. He'd apparently told Miss Baker about her threat to take the children.

Julia talked about how much she loved to teach and how she was so blessed to be in this town because they helped her with whatever she needed. In fact, Joshua had helped her many times. She went on and on about how Seth was the ideal student, and she was sure Rebecca and Emily would follow his example.

Anna took a bite of her roll with a little more enthusiasm than normal. "I'm sure Joshua is extremely helpful when he has time. From what I've observed the ranch keeps him occupied."

"You've only experienced what it's like during the summer. In the fall and winter, everything slows down. I've been to the ranch many fall evenings and watched the children play games with Joshua. We all sat on the front porch while a slight breeze whispered through the trees. It was so lovely. And when the sun set, we searched for constellations, sipped hot chocolate and simply enjoyed the children's laughter. I look forward to more of those times." Julia looked at Joshua and smiled.

Luke stood up and held his hand out to Anna. "Well, ladies, I don't know about you, but I'm ready for dessert. Why don't you show me which pies you and Mrs. Brown made, Miss Wilson?"

Anna took his hand. "I'd love too. Excuse us."

Luke led Anna to the food tables. "What was that about?"

"I told Mr. Brown if he didn't find help for his mother, I'd have to place Seth and Rebecca with another family. Miss Baker wants me to understand what an amazing father he is, and she has a prior claim on him." Anna pointed to an empty pie tin and another one which had two pieces left. "There's what's left of our pies."

"Whoa, you said you'd take Seth and Rebecca away?" Luke looked incredulous. "Mr. Brown is one of the best fathers I've been around."

Anna put the last two pieces of pie on Luke's plate. "I agree, he is a good father. But he also has a lot of responsibility, and Mrs. Brown can't keep up with three young children and a big house. Ella and I work all day to do what he expects his mother to do alone. I don't know how much longer I'll be here, and Mrs. Brown's arm isn't completely healed."

"I'm surprised he didn't tell you to leave instead of asking you to move in." Luke took a bite of the pie. "This is good."

"Thank you. I think he knew I was right." Anna looked back to where Joshua and Julia sat under the tree. Clara had left to talk with her friends, and the children were off playing again, except for Emily who sat on Julia's lap. Luke ate the last bite of his pie. Anna didn't relish spending any more time with Julia. She slid two rolls into her pocket. Luke raised his eyebrows in a question. "The children like to feed the ducks." Anna untied her bonnet and took it off. Her head was pounding, and she wanted to feel the cool breeze.

"If my intuition is correct," she said as she took Luke's arm, "I'd say you'd rather be sharing this occasion with Miss Baker. Have you two been courting?" Anna tried to read Luke's reaction.

"We went to a few dances together. I thought Julia liked me, but whenever she's around Mr. Brown, she acts like they're a couple. I don't know why she was claiming she'd been to the ranch a lot. I think she's only been there once, and she came with another lady from church with a covered dish. Mr. Brown hasn't paid her much notice until today. I had hoped she'd give up on him and realize I'm her best choice." Luke laughed. "Why should I care, though? I have the prettiest woman right here by my side."

"I have to warn you, I don't want a man in my life. I'm fine with being labeled a spinster." Anna took a roll from her pocket and tore it apart. "And you care because you like her."

"You're way too pretty to be a spinster, and if I can't win your heart, I bet one of these other men can. If you'd get Mr. Brown's attention, it might help us all." Luke winked at her.

Anna punched his arm. "You're awful."

"Actually, I'm quite nice, Ma'am." Luke grinned. He threw pieces of the roll to the ducks swimming in the lake. It didn't take long before all the children surrounded him. Anna had to hand over her roll and go back for more.

~

When they got back to the ranch, Joshua helped Clara down and then held his hand out to Anna. She took his hand. Warmth flowed through her as she climbed down from the wagon. She cleared her throat, hoping to dispel the heat. She wiped her hands on her skirt. "I'm going to see the Weavers today." She knew if she waited until the next day they wouldn't be there.

As much as she wanted to follow Joshua into the house, she had to go today.

"Henry Weaver is not a pleasant man. Miss Baker informed me at the potluck she went out to visit Mr. and Mrs. Weaver because the boys weren't in school. Mr. Weaver ran her off, and she never got to see the boys. I'd go with you but I need to check on a couple of sick cows in the upper pasture. You can ask Luke to go."

Miss Baker again. Anna thought they had left all talk of her back at the potluck. Well, she had hoped. Anna walked to the front of the wagon. "The Weavers aren't required by law to attend school in Texas, but the Children's Aid Society makes that a condition of taking responsibility of a child. All children in New York City have had to attend school for almost twenty years now." Although Luke's company would be helpful, Anna didn't want to give him false hope. "I'm sure I'll be fine. I have to go today, or it will be another week before I see them."

"I wish you'd listen to me, but since you won't, I'll have Luke water the horses and harness them to the buggy before you leave." Joshua walked toward the barn, his shoulders back and a little extra stomp in his step.

~

Anna's stomach clutched as if it had fifty knots in it by the time she turned down the track to the Weaver farm. Not one thing moved in the yard, the same as last time. Anna stopped the horses in front of the house. "Hello, is anyone here," she yelled.

Silence.

She got down from the buggy and knocked on the front door. "Hello, is anyone home? This is Miss Wilson from the Children's Aid Society, and I'm here to talk with Jack and Noah."

"What are you doing here?" A man yelled as he came around the corner of the house. "My missus told you the boys are fine and you shouldn't come back?"

Anna jumped. She whirled to find the face of a bearded man scowling at her. Dirt smudged every inch of his face. His dark brown eyes pierced her like a sword. She felt the impact all the way to her toes.

"Hello, I'm Miss Wilson." Anna stammered. She stuck out her hand, but Mr. Weaver didn't move. "Are you Mr. Weaver? Your wife assured me the boys were doing all right, but I have to see them and report back to the orphanage. It's part of the agreement you made when you offered to take responsibility of them. If you won't let me see them today, then I'll get the sheriff and be back tomorrow."

"I'm Henry Weaver." He smirked. "They're busy."

He can't notice how nervous I am. I have to stand up to him. "Would you please get them?" Anna stood as tall as she could, but 5'4" was no match for his six-foot frame.

"I'll fetch them from the barn. You have five minutes." Mr. Weaver sauntered off.

"It may take longer than that." Anna called to his back.

"I make the rules here, Miss Wilson. I said five minutes." Mr. Weaver yelled. "Jack! Noah! Get out here. A nosy woman wants to see you."

Two skinny boys peeked around the barn door. They dragged their feet in the dirt with their heads down until they stood in front of Mr. Weaver. He whispered to them and put a hand on each boys shoulder. They walked over to Anna. Jack had a black eye. Noah kept looking at Mr. Weaver and then at the ground. Jack walked straight ahead, eyes boring through her.

"I'd rather speak with the boys alone." Anna said.

"I'm sorry that is what you'd rather do, but I'll be here with them. I don't want no city woman putting notions in their head." Mr. Weaver stared at Anna.

"Is your wife here?" Anna asked.

"She went to visit her sister." Weaver spat a stream of tobacco in front of Anna's shoes.

"How are you boys?" Anna looked at each of them. "I'm Miss Wilson from the Children's Aid Society, and I'm here to see if you're happy living with the Weavers."

"Sure." Jack looked down and drew lines in the dirt with the toe of his boot.

"Yeah." Noah said and glanced at Mr. Weaver.

"How'd you get that black eye, Jack?" Anna asked.

"Umm... ran into a post in the barn not watching where I was goin'." Jack looked up and stared at Anna.

"Are you getting enough food to eat? Your clothes look too small, and you need new shoes as your toes are sticking out of them." Anna wanted to hug both boys. She could tell they were lying and Jack seemed to dare her to help them.

"You've been here long enough. They eat, have a place to sleep and there's nothing wrong with their shoes." Mr. Weaver turned the boys around with his hands.

"Wait! You don't understand, Mr. Weaver. You're

not taking care of them how you agreed to. I need to place them with another family." Jack turned his head back toward Anna and for the first time she saw life in his eyes.

Mr. Weaver turned around. "No, I don't think you understand. These boys ain't going nowhere. I need them on this farm. We give them food and a place to live. Get in your buggy and go back to New York City. They won't be leaving here."

"I won't leave here without them." Anna glared at Mr. Weaver.

"I can put you in your buggy, if you don't do it yourself. Boys, go to the barn." Noah and Jack ran to the barn. "What will it be?"

"I'll leave for now, but I promise to be back with the sheriff. Those boys deserve much more than you're providing for them." Anna returned to the buggy, climbed up and sat down.

"I thought you'd see it my way, and I'd be careful on who you threaten. Best get on that train and head back where you came from." Weaver turned around and strode toward the barn.

"I'd be careful who *you* threaten, Mr. Weaver. The law is on my side." Anna flipped the reins and turned the horses toward the path.

Anna couldn't concentrate on the ride home. Her heart was racing. She wanted to punch something. The boys weren't being cared for, and she'd bet Mr. Weaver was hitting Jack. She noticed a curtain move inside their house when she left. Mrs. Weaver must've been there. The man was a liar, a bully and who knew what else. She'd have to go back to the ranch tonight as the sun was setting. *First thing in the morning, I'm going to town and getting the sheriff.* Anna should've listened to Joshua and let Luke go with her. She might have had the boys with her if she had. Instead, she'd been jealous when he brought up Miss Baker and let her pride get in the way.

Bang!

Something whizzed past her and the horses broke into a run. *Was that a bullet?* She yanked on the reins as hard as she could, but the horses wouldn't slow down. They went faster and faster. The buggy struck a boulder and Anna flew through the air. Her head hit something, and it seemed to be on fire, just as everything went black.

Chapter Eight

At the end of the day, Joshua and five of his men rode into the yard and dismounted. Pieces of a buggy lay in front of the barn. *It had to be the buggy Anna took.* He shouted for Luke, but Jake came around the corner of the barn. He told Joshua that Luke took three of the men and rode out when the horses raced into the yard pulling the remains of the buggy. Jake also sent Ben for the doctor, just in case. Joshua reeled his horse around to the gate. A dust cloud was forming in the distance. Two riders rode hard for the ranch. Luke wasn't with them.

"Did you find Miss Wilson?" Joshua asked.

Steven pulled his horse up and patted the neck of the lathered animal. "Luke's with Miss Wilson. She's unconscious and lost a lot of blood. She was thrown from the buggy and hit her head on a rock. He bandaged her head up as well as he could. He's behind us, riding slowly so he won't jostle her much. He sent us to go for the doctor and to let ya'll know what's going on."

Joshua wiped the sweat from his creased forehead. "The doc's on his way. Is anyone riding with Luke?"

"Colt is, he's our best shooter. Guess we'll rub down the horses unless you need us to do something else?" Steven dismounted.

Joshua gave his reins to Jim and asked him to take care of his horse. He went into the house. His mother needed to know what happened, and she would have to prepare a place for Anna. *Why didn't I send someone with her? I shouldn't have let her make that decision. She doesn't understand the dangers.* He wondered if Weaver had played a part in this. If so, he would be sorry.

~

Joshua paced back and forth on the front porch, watching the horizon for Luke and Anna. It felt like an eternity but hadn't been more than thirty minutes since Steven rode in. Finally, he caught sight of two riders in the distance. Luke rode up with Anna in front of him. He had his arms around her to keep her on the horse. Her head hung forward, and she wasn't moving. Blood showed through the bandage Luke had tied around her head.

"How is she?" Joshua asked as Luke handed her down to him.

"Miss Wilson hasn't moved since we found her. She's breathing, but she has lost a lot of blood." Luke got off his horse and followed Joshua up the porch steps. "Let me get the door."

"Why don't you wait in the dining room? I want to talk about what you saw after I get her settled." Joshua carried Anna to Ella's room. Clara and the kids waited for them there.

"Is Miss Wilson going to be all right?" Ella asked as Joshua laid Anna on the bed.

"I hope so. She was thrown off the buggy and hit her head." Joshua looked at the anxious little faces around him. He didn't feel he had enough faith to pray for her healing. The last time he'd prayed for God to heal a woman in this house, it didn't end so well. Tears ran down Ella's cheeks.

Luke pushed into the room with the doctor on his heels. Doc Fisher wanted to know what happened. Clara left with the children so the men could talk. Luke told him how he'd found her and what he did.

"It's good you got the bleeding stopped," the doctor said, looking at the wound on Anna's head. "The cut doesn't look deep but head wounds bleed a lot. It will require stitches." He looked up from his work to the two men standing over him. "Why don't you gentlemen send Mrs. Brown in here? I need to check for other injuries." The doctor raised his eyebrow.

Joshua felt his face get warm as he followed Luke. They found Clara in the kitchen. "Mother, Doc Fisher needs your help. He wants you in there while he examines Anna."

Clara had given the children cookies and milk. Joshua knew from his childhood that cookies and milk were meant to make everything better. The children sat around the table completely quiet except for Ella, who was sobbing. Joshua sent Luke to find Jim. He wanted to meet with them.

Joshua sat at the table with the children. "What kind of cookies are you eating?"

"Father, will Miss Wilson be all right?" Seth asked.

"She has to get better. No one else loves me." Big

tears streamed down Ella's cheeks.

Joshua drew Ella into a hug. "The doctor is checking her. He'll do everything he can to see she gets better. Ella, you have us and we all love you."

Luke and Jim clomped into the kitchen but stopped when they saw the turmoil of the children. They waited until Ella settled down and followed Joshua into the dining room.

"I want to give you both more responsibilities. Jim, I want you to be my cattle foreman. Luke, I want you to be the horse and ranch foreman. With Miss Wilson hurt, and my mother's arm still not completely better, I will have to help her with the children. I want you both to run the day's plans by me each morning but making sure it gets done will be up to the two of you. I'll double your pay." Joshua pushed a plate of cookies toward Luke and Jim. "Help yourselves and let me know if you want to do this."

Without any need to consider the offer, both men welcomed the added responsibilities. Luke remembered the mail he held inside his shirt and gave it to Joshua. There was a letter addressed to Anna. The Children's Aid Society had forwarded it. There wasn't a name on it, only a return address. Joshua drummed the letter against his hand, wondering if he should open it or not.

~

Joshua sat in the corner of the room, he'd only left one lantern glowing by Anna's bedside. The doctor had left hours earlier and his mother and he were planning on taking turns sitting with her. They'd had dinner, and the children were asleep. Joshua shooed his mother off to bed and settled in for the first watch.

Even with Luke and Jim taking on new

responsibilities, he needed more help. In the soft light of the lantern, he wrote to Lizzy, asking for her help for a few days.

Ella snuck in when she thought everyone had left. She gave Anna a kiss on the cheek and said a quick prayer. She never even noticed Joshua in the corner. He'd never admit it, but a tear escaped the corner of his eye. He got up and moved his chair by Anna's bedside. Doc Fisher had stitched and bandaged the cut on her head. He hadn't found any other injuries.

Anna's long eyelashes rested on her cheeks, and Joshua wished she would open her eyes. There was nothing he wanted more than to see those pretty hazel eyes and know she was okay. He watched every breath and touched her forehead, checking for the fever the doctor warned Joshua about.

His thoughts drifted to the night he'd kissed Anna. He could care for this woman. He probably already did. But every time he let himself think that way, guilt at letting Sarah's memory go consumed him. Sarah had been happy, bubbly, and full of life. Anna was a mystery, a force which ran swift and passionate. She was protective of the children in her care. Although in his case, she'd misjudged him. He would never put his children at risk.

Joshua wondered how it had gone at the Weaver's. Maybe he should send Steven to get the sheriff. He should definitely question Henry Weaver. The thought left Joshua unsettled. He touched Anna's forehead again and let his hand linger on her cheek. *She's a beautiful woman, even with a bandage wrapped around her head.* Joshua smiled. He didn't understand why she'd never married. She must have shut herself off from the outside world. He understood how painful love could be. He'd promised himself never to marry after Sarah died. Would she have wanted that?

"Pray for her, Joshua."

"Who said that?" Joshua looked around, but no one was there.

"Trust Me."

Joshua felt God's presence in the room. He prayed for God to heal her, to comfort her and to bring her back to them. Joshua's faith had taken a hit when Sarah died, but he did what God prompted him to. Joshua held Anna's hand while he prayed, and now it didn't feel right to let go. He laid his head on the bed next to her. He'd just rest for a second.

Chapter Nine

Anna's heart raced as she pried her eyes open. The room spun when she tried to move. Her head pounded. Why had she slept in Ella's room? Joshua's head rested on the bed and he held onto her hand.

Anna tried talking, but her parched mouth made working her tongue impossible. She squeezed Joshua's hand, but he didn't move. Anna touched a bandage wrapping on her head. *What happened?* Anna squeezed Joshua's hand harder. He stirred and sat up.

"You're awake. Thank you, Father." Joshua let go of her hand, his face turning pink. "How are you?"

Anna wasn't sure what she wanted more, his hand or a glass of water. "Water, please." Anna whispered.

Joshua poured water from the bedside table into a cup. He helped her sit up and drink. Anna took two long sips. Joshua asked her what she remembered. Anna recalled being at the church potluck but nothing after that. Her stomach felt queasy and the room wouldn't stop spinning.

Joshua reminded her that she took the buggy to the

Weavers after the potluck. She looked confused when he told her. The horses and part of the buggy returned to the ranch a few hours later. He didn't want to distress her, but he needed to know what she remembered, so he told her how Luke had found her lying in the dirt next to a boulder. "Doc sewed you up, and we've been waiting for you to wake up."

"Did something scare the horses?" Anna asked.

"That would be my guess. I'm thankful you're all right. I better wake up Mother and the children. They were very worried about you." Joshua got up.

"Thank you for staying with me. I'm sorry I upset everyone." Anna shut her eyes.

"Why don't you rest before I bring them all in here to see you?" Joshua closed the door quietly behind him.

~

Joshua picked Anna up off the bed and carried her out to the porch swing. It had been three days since the accident, but she still had bad headaches and dizziness. The doctor said the fresh air would be beneficial for her, but she shouldn't walk without help.

Joshua's heart beat against her side as he held her. He smelled of the outdoors and the ease in which he carried her proved hard work paid off. She wished she could stay in the comfort of his arms, protected and cherished. She appreciated everything he'd done for her, and he'd proven his children came before the ranch. After all, he was home helping Clara and her. It got harder each day to keep her wall of indifference up. But Anna couldn't let her guard down, or she might care too much.

The sheriff had come by and talked with her and then went out to the Weaver's. Weaver said she was fine when she'd left their farm.

He had Luke show him where he found Anna, but Sheriff Allen didn't come across anything suspicious there either.

Joshua sat her in the swing. "Do you need anything else?"

Anna pushed her hair out of her face. The breeze blew it everywhere. "I'm sorry, I need a blanket? I should've grabbed the one on my bed, but I got so excited about coming outside, I forgot it."

"Of course." Joshua went back into the house.

Her room had become a prison. She wanted the dizziness and headaches to go away so she could get up. She closed her eyes against the memory of the spinning room. Instead, she remembered the visit by Pastor Smith and his wife the day before. They had brought Laura to cheer her. Seeing her do so well with her new family did provide comfort to Anna. Laura gave her a bouquet of roses. She'd been all smiles with stories of her new life with the Smiths. If only all children could be so lucky. A tear slipped from Anna's eyes as she gazed up at the sky. The stars shone bright. *Did God exist in that vast universe?*

"Here's your blanket." Joshua draped the blanket around her shoulders and sat in the rocking chair. "Oh, I almost forgot, this letter arrived for you." Joshua pulled it out of his shirt pocket.

Anna took the envelope. There was no name just a return address, but that address she would never forget. *Bennett. Why is he writing me?* Anna opened the envelope and took the page out.

Dearest Anna,

This letter will be a shock to you. I'm sorry for what I did eight years ago. I'm sure you felt I used you, but that's not the real story. What took place between us meant as much to me as it did to you. I loved you, Anna. I still do. You won't believe it, but it's true. I didn't mean for that night to happen. I took advantage of your inexperience and vulnerability and it weighs on me. I should've married you, and because I didn't, I will always live with that regret.

Not only did I love you but my children loved you. They cried for days and wouldn't talk to me after you left. They still ask about you. I made the biggest mistake of my life when I told you to leave us, but there are so many things you were unaware of.

I had spent all my inheritance. The people I owed money to demanded I sell everything to pay my debts. I kept a big part of my life secret. I had a sickness which controlled me, gambling. I started before you came to work for us, and I continued up until last year. All of those late night meetings were poker games.

I had to get a large sum of money fast, so I made the only choice that would work, Miss Anderson. She never hid her interest in me. She flirted with me at every dinner party I went to. I had kissed her a few times, and she told me she wanted us to court. I've done bad things in my life but what I did to her and to you were the worst. I asked her father for permission to marry her and then proposed. I paid off my debts once we married, but I kept gambling. She had to go to her father a few years later to ask for more money, because, again, I had acquired a large amount of debt. She died in childbirth last year. I lost her and our baby. I didn't love her when we married, but I grew to love her.

The children and I are living in an apartment, although, they are not so young now. I have a job I go to every day. I gave up gambling and for the first time in many years I am not being controlled by a sickness.

I learned from an old friend that you worked at the orphanage. I'm not surprised you are working with children. You are a wonderful woman. I want to do what's right by you Anna, even if it's eight years too late. I want to marry you, so we can be a family. I love you and I'm sorry for hurting you.

Forever yours,
Bennett

Anna laid the letter down with trembling hands. Tears ran down her cheeks. The words she'd hoped to hear eight years ago were written on the crinkled page in her lap. She'd given herself to a man she believed loved her. Her desperation had led her to do things she shouldn't have. "Are you all right?" Joshua asked.

"I will be. Ghosts that have been lain to rest are painful to face when resurrected." Anna put the letter back into the envelope.

"If you want to talk about it, I'm a great listener." Joshua leaned over and took hold of her hand. "Maybe I should have waited a few more days to give it to you."

Anna's heart raced at his touch. "I'm all right. Thank you for giving the letter to me. I need to tell you about my past, but my story isn't for young ears. Is Clara and Lizzy putting the children to bed?"

"Yes, they told me to take you outside and relax. If you're tired, we can do this discussion another time." Joshua's voice soothed Anna's nerves.

"I'm tired but I'll never want to have this conversation. I need to tell you the entire truth on why I left my nanny position with Bennett North. He did tell me to leave, and he married another woman, but I didn't tell you why he wanted me to leave.

"He asked me to be a nanny for him after my parent's death as a favor to his father. My father and Bennett's father had been close since childhood. I was only seventeen, homesick and sad. I enjoyed watching the children because it kept my mind off missing my parents. The first three years, I seldom saw Bennett. He entertained guests or spent his nights away. When he was with the children, I would leave them alone. I only truly spent time with him on holidays, birthdays or an outing. He was courteous, but withdrawn. Things changed the last year.

"He made a point of being with us. He spoke to me when the children were playing, and he seemed genuinely interested in me. We became friends. I let myself dream of what a future would be like with him.

"I loved reading in the library after the children went to bed. One night he came in and asked me to help him pick out a good book. I searched the shelves to locate my favorite book. He came up behind me, and I could feel his breath on my neck. I'd never been that close to a man. When I turned around, I found myself in his arms. He drew me close and kissed me. I smelled alcohol and I didn't know how to react to his kiss. Should I slap him? He might fire me. Instead, I pushed him aside and ran upstairs to my room."

Joshua still held her hand but the other hand was clenched. "I convinced myself he must be in love with me. He pursued me and tried to find me alone. He would touch my cheek or hold me close. Eventually, I accepted his kisses. I was confident he wanted to marry me. I didn't understand the unlikelihood of a rich man marrying his nanny. Men like Bennett may use nannies as their mistresses, but they weren't good enough to be their wives. I knew none of that. My parents had sheltered me from the realities of the world in which we lived."

Joshua let go of her hand and sat up in the rocking chair. Anna missed the strength his touch gave her, but she didn't blame him. "When he didn't ask me to marry him, I became worried. I thought no other man would want me because I'd allowed Bennett to kiss me. I couldn't lose him. I didn't have anyone else. My only option was to show him how much I loved him. He would have to marry me then. I don't think I fully understood what I was offering him, but that's no excuse. I waited in his room one night with pictures the children drew. It was a pretty naïve thing to do. The next morning before everyone woke up I snuck back to my room. I wanted to hide. I had let him have my most precious gift. I'd made a bad decision."

Joshua turned his head away and Anna couldn't see how he was reacting to what she just said. "A few days later he announced his engagement to Miss Anderson and told me to pack my bags and move out. I walked by the orphanage and noticed a help-wanted sign. I applied and got a cleaning job. I worked hard and eventually became an agent. I never heard from Bennett again until now." Anna held the letter out to Joshua. "Please read it. I want you to know everything." Anna gave the lantern sitting beside her to him.

Joshua read the letter and gave it back to Anna. She had watched him intently as he read it. Not a muscle in his face moved but his hand had clenched again.

"I'm sorry I didn't tell you the first night you asked. I haven't been alone with another man until I came here. I decided to live my life as a spinster. I wanted to punish myself for what I did." Anna's tears continued to fall.

"His words made you cry. Do you still love him?" Joshua asked.

"The tears were from reading the words I'd hoped to hear eight years ago. I'm not in love with him anymore." Anna gazed up at the sky. The stars were so beautiful and the breeze so refreshing, she could pretend she hadn't just shut a door with Joshua that they could never open. *How could he look at her the same after all that she said?*

"I should get you inside. I'm sure you're worn out." Joshua picked Anna up in his arms and carried her through the house. "Try to rest now. Your body needs sleep to get better." Joshua closed the door behind him as he walked out.

He hadn't commented on anything she'd told him. Regret and sorrow crushed down on her. Joshua Brown's opinion was way more important than it should be. Anna glanced out her window at the moon, no matter where someone lived they all saw the same yellow ball of light. The white chintz curtains blew toward her and then retreated as the breeze left. The soft movement of the air did little to dissipate the suffocating humidity. Tears trickled down her cheeks as she touched the bandage on her head. Her life continued to rotate around the choices she'd made eight years ago. She thought she had fixed it, but mistakes never went away.

In the days to come, Anna watched the family work together from her bed. Ella especially amazed Anna. The young girl gave to everyone and simply wanted love in return. Anna understood those feelings well. Not having anyone to belong to was scary. Anna didn't want Ella to make decisions she would regret for the rest of her life because she felt alone. She needed to find a way for her and Ella to become a family.

Chapter Ten

Joshua walked through fields of grass toward the pond as the cattle grazed. Clouds gathered in the west, but the morning had been full of sunshine. Tall pine trees shaded the pond as fish jumped, hoping to get the unlucky bug that landed on the water. Joshua was at peace for the first time in days. It had been three weeks since Anna's accident. Her headaches and dizziness had subsided, and she was glad to be able to help his mother since Lizzy had left to go back home to her husband.

Joshua hadn't spoken more than a few words to Anna since she told him the truth of her relationship with Bennett. He understood the desperation which led her to the choices she made and why she'd been scared to tell him. When he read the letter from Bennett North, he'd wanted to punch the guy. Still, it bothered him more than it should have when Anna spoke of the love she'd had for him.

Joshua had vowed to never marry again after Sarah died. He couldn't imagine loving anyone the way he had loved her. She'd been his best friend for as long as he remembered. He realized he was in love with her when they took a walk after her seventeenth birthday dinner. They strolled by the creek that flowed through her parent's property, just as they had done many times. This occasion was different. When he gazed at her in the moonlight, he knew he loved her. How could anything that had happened so naturally be topped? It was better not to try.

They'd had a good life together even though it was much shorter than he hoped for. He had worked hard the last two years to build a wall around his heart. Joshua had believed it was impenetrable.

Anna was beautiful, and Joshua found her charming. She was strong yet sensitive. He hadn't met anyone as devoted to the needs of children as she was. Anna allowed them full access to her heart. They trusted her because of that and opened themselves up to her.

A blast of wind blew Joshua's hat off his head. He picked it up and looked up. The sky was a steely gray. *When did those clouds drift in?* It was as dark as twilight, and it couldn't be later than three. A gust pressed against his chest. He had to get to the ranch. He met up with Jim and two of his men, who had been working at the lower pasture.

"The weather's looking bad, boss." Jim rode up. "We might be in for a tornado."

"I thought the same thing. Get everyone into the storm cellars and pray the livestock will survive." Joshua pushed his horse to gallop faster.

Rain and hail pelted Joshua as they reached the house. He dismounted and handed the reins to Jim. "Put the horses in the corral and get everyone into the cellar." Joshua looked toward the roiling sky. A cloud, like a hand, reached toward the ground. Tumble weeds bounced through the yard. "There's a big funnel cloud forming. It's coming the same way we did, straight toward the ranch."

Joshua rang the warning bell. He ran into the house. "Everyone, get to the storm cellar now! A tornado is coming!"

Clara rushed into the room with the children behind her. "Anna and Ella are in the garden."

Joshua picked up Emily, grabbed Rebecca's hand and pulled her through the house. He opened the storm cellar door so they could climb down. "Get the kids in, Mother. I'm going after Anna and Ella."

Anna and Ella were running toward the house but the hail and wind were pushing against them.

"A tornado is coming," Joshua yelled.

He grasped their hands and pulled them through the gusting wind toward the cellar door, praying they'd make it in time. He climbed down the ladder last and tried to close the hatch but the wind was too strong. "Anna, grab that rope and hand it to me." He put it through the handle and let the end fall to the cellar floor. "Everyone, pull!" The door snapped shut as they all helped. Joshua latched it and tied the rope around barrels of flour and sugar.

The deafening noise grew in intensity, and the cellar door banged up and down. Clara fumbled with matches in the suffocating darkness and finally lit a couple of candles. The children were crying so Anna and Ella put their arms around them.

Clara prayed. "Jesus, protect us in this storm. Calm our fears and help us feel Your presence." Emily stopped crying and snuggled into her Grandmother.

"Son, did all the men get into their cellar?" Clara asked.

"I believe so. Most of them were in when I ran to help Anna and Ella." Joshua held the end of the rope as a last resort.

The roar intensified. He wanted to shout encouragement to his family, but he would not be heard over the wind. While it seemed much longer, the wind died down in only a few minutes.

Ella tried to squeeze past Clara to get to the ladder. Clara stepped in her way and told her she had to wait until the men made sure the tornado was past.

Joshua climbed the ladder and lifted the door for a cautious look. Ella was right behind him. The wind wasn't gusting, so he pushed it open. Luke and Jim headed toward their cellar. Already the clouds parted to reveal a blue sky. Joshua turned slowly to assess any damage. The house still stood. The tornado only tore a few sections of the roof off. Wood and shingles covered the ground.

Anna stood next to him holding Emily. "How often do you have tornados?"

"Too often, I guess." He met her eyes and saw the worry there. "We can go years without a tornado or have two or three in a month. There's no way to tell. We've never had a tornado this close to the ranch, though."

The tornado had skirted the ranch, so the damage was less than it could've been. The horses remained safe in the corrals, which was a great grace. And except for some roof damage, the house was intact. The bunkhouse saw the worst of it. The roof ripped off. It lay upended on the ground past the corrals, but still intact. The men ran their hands over the horses, up and down their legs and along their sides, checking for wounds in need of treatment. They'd ride out tomorrow and check the cattle. It would take time to fix everything but everything was fixable. For that Joshua was grateful.

~

They worked the rest of the afternoon repairing the roof on the house and cleaning up the mess inside from the rain and hail. Once Anna and Clara had the kitchen clean, they set to fixing supper for the tired workers.

At the dinner table, Joshua bowed his head and thanked God for protecting them through the tornado. Clara asked for help to carry the food in from the kitchen. Luke and two other men got up.

Joshua poured himself a cup of coffee from the kettle. "Jim, did Luke say why he hadn't noticed the storm before we rode up?"

"They were in the barn mucking out the stalls and assumed a rainstorm was passing through. When they heard us ride up, they thought something must be wrong, so Ben stepped outside. He saw the tornado and told Luke. Luke was yelling for everyone to get in the cellar by the time I got to the barn. It was a rush, but we made it. We sure need a stronger latch for the cellar doors." Jim took a sip of coffee.

"I agree. I had a hard time getting ours shut and latched. The door over the bunkhouse cellar is even heavier. And we need a backup plan if something breaks."

Anna walked into the dining room, carrying two bowls piled high with rolls. Luke held a big pot of either soup or stew. "It looks like we'll be eating well tonight thanks to my mother, Anna and Ella," Joshua said.

"For sure." Luke winked at Anna. "It was all I could do to resist eating a roll before we brought them out. You'll want to save room for desert, though. What I observed in the kitchen will make your mouth water. I don't know how Miss Wilson managed to bake this afternoon, but I can't wait to taste it."

Anna's cheeks turned pink. Joshua wondered if something was going on between her and Luke. They'd spent a lot of time together at the church potluck. Joshua had watched them walking by the lake as Miss Baker had talked on and on about the newest dress designs. And Luke had rescued Anna after the accident. He'd even checked on her a couple of times when she'd been recovering. He wouldn't blame Luke if he found Anna attractive. She could steal a man's heart before he understood what was going on.

Luke was a good man. He deserved any happiness life brought him. If Anna returned his affection, why shouldn't they build a life together. That's why Joshua wouldn't let any cracks open in the wall around his heart.

Dinner was delicious. Everyone ate until they were full and then ate more. Luke was right, the cherry pie was worth having a second piece. His mother cooked excellent meals, but Anna had a way with desserts.

The men crowded together in the living room by the warmth of the fire after dinner. They were ready to play cards for a few hours. Joshua had warned them there would be no gambling in the house. His mother took the children upstairs to get them ready for bed while

Anna finished cleaning in the kitchen. Joshua heard the screen door close, so he went outside to see who left.

When he walked outside, Joshua found Anna and Luke talking as they looked up at the sky. "It's good to see a sky full of stars. A welcome sign after this afternoon." Joshua walked over to the porch rail near Luke.

"I'd jump up and down in a mud hole, if it meant I never went through another tornado." Anna said.

"No one ever wants to see a funnel forming in the clouds." Luke looked around. "We have a lot of repairs, but I'm glad all the animals were fine. Even our newest addition, the colt who still needs a name."

Anna glanced at Joshua when Luke mentioned the colt. "Why don't we call him, Tornado. That seems fitting." Anna looked back to Luke and smiled.

Luke grinned back at Anna. "Tornado, I like it. Let's hope it's not an indication of how difficult he'll be to break. I'm glad all the livestock on the ranch made it through the tornado without any major injuries. I hope the cattle fair as well. Are you checking them tomorrow?"

"Jim and I will be heading out early. Get the men working on the bunkhouse first. Then we'll repair the barn. The mothers need a safe place to have their little ones." Joshua kept his gaze on Anna as he tilted his chair to balance on two legs.

Luke shook his head. "We should wait on the bunkhouse. I'll enjoy the sleeping arrangements tonight, as it's been awhile since I've slept in a house. The food definitely beats Hank's. He cooks all right, but it doesn't have that special woman's touch. Can you imagine ol' Hank baking us a cherry pie?" Luke laughed.

"I don't think that will happen any time soon. Maybe Miss Wilson would make y'all a dessert once a week." Joshua smiled at Anna.

"I should have thought of that." Anna said.

Luke rubbed his stomach. "I'll look forward to more cherry pies from you, Miss Wilson. Fact is, you could sell your baked goods in town. They're better than anything they offer there." He took off his hat and raked his hands through his hair. "Looking at the wood and junk lying everywhere reminds me of all the work we have to do tomorrow. Morning will come soon enough. Tonight, I'm going to join the card game." Luke patted Joshua on the shoulder and went inside.

"Is Luke interested in you?" Joshua didn't realize he blurted out his thoughts until it was too late.

"Not in the way you're thinking. Luke is like a brother to me. He likes to joke around and we talk, but that's it. He has his eye on the school teacher, Miss Baker. They went to a couple of dances together, but Luke said she has her sights on you."

"Really? Miss Baker? I hadn't noticed. Other than the church potluck, I've hardly spoken with her." Joshua shifted, looked at his boots. "I owe you a response to what you shared with me about your past. Do you think we could go for a walk?" Joshua asked.

Anna grabbed her shawl. Joshua led her toward the pond where they wouldn't be disturbed. They walked in silence but the sounds of the card game could still be heard all the way there. He was sure his mother must be happy about that. Joshua and Anna sat on the wooden bench he had made for Sarah. His thigh touched Anna's thigh. He should have made the bench wider. Being so close to her didn't help him keep his thoughts on what he wanted to say.

He started with the obvious. "Thank you for being honest with me about your past. It gave me a lot to think about," Joshua pressed toward the arm of the bench to gain some space between him and Anna.

"I understand." Anna's eyes glistened with unshed tears.

"Don't get upset. I understand why you made the choices you did. We all make mistakes. I've made plenty. I wouldn't hold it against you. You love unconditionally, Anna. I see it in how you are with the children. I'm certain you did the same with Bennett, even though he didn't deserve it. I'd never treat a woman the way he did you. My parents raised me to respect women." Joshua looked out at the pond. The water was still, not a hint of the wind which blew through earlier. The moon's yellow light danced across the water as the crickets chirruped all around them.

"I was so naïve." Anna pushed a couple of loose curls behind her ear. "I wish that night had never happened. I fear no man will ever want me as his wife."

"If a man loves you, he'll forgive most anything. Most men have done far more than you did. I'm not saying what you did was right, but none of us should judge you. Society looks at it differently, but I don't." Joshua ran his fingers through his hair pushing it back from his face.

Anna looked at the ground, working the corner of her shawl between her fingers. "Thank you for saying that, but even you wouldn't want me to be a mother to your children, no respectable man would. I accepted that a long time ago. I have Ella, and we'll be fine."

Joshua tilted her head up to look at him. "You have been taking care of my children as a mother would. Ella isn't the only one who loves you Anna. You have a heavenly Father who does. He's waiting for you to find your way back to him." Joshua put his arm around her shoulders. He shouldn't have done that. Something happened when he touched Anna that drove all thoughts but her from his head.

"I wish I could believe it, but I can't." Anna sobbed.

"It's the truth." Joshua pulled her close to his side, and she laid her head on his chest. "He never stops loving us."

Anna closed her eyes. Joshua kissed her on the forehead. He wiped the tears from her cheeks. She shivered. He wondered if she was cold or feeling the same things he was. Joshua wanted to kiss her like he had the night in the barn, but he wouldn't lead her on. Anna had many redeeming qualities, but getting involved with someone who couldn't forgive herself or God was a bad idea.

Joshua stood and offered Anna a helping hand. "Let's go back to the house."

They walked back to the house with a wide distance between them. At the back door, Anna stopped. "I'm going to sit on the porch for a few minutes before I go in."

"See you in the morning." Joshua went into the house. The screen door banged shut. He had closed the door on any thoughts of a relationship with Anna. He felt empty and knew sleep would be an elusive hope tonight.

Chapter Eleven

Dust billowed in the distance from a lone rider approaching the ranch. Anna sat on the porch swing, resting after a busy morning of cleaning and baking. Inside, Clara taught Ella to sew while the younger girls took a nap. Anna shielded her eyes from the sun's glare, but she couldn't make out who the rider was. Luke must have noticed the rider, too, because he was walking toward her.

"Who is it?" Anna asked Luke as he climbed the steps.

"Looks like the sheriff. He's the only one I know who sits a Paint." Luke sat in the chair next to Anna.

Sheriff Allen rode up and tied his horse to the hitching post. He looked around at the damage the tornado had done. "Anyone hurt?" he asked. Luke told him everyone made it to the cellars. After he questioned Luke about the damage to the buildings, he asked to speak to Joshua.

Luke and Anna shared a questioning look. "What's wrong, Sheriff?" Luke asked. "Joshua won't be back for a couple of hours. He's checking the cattle to see if any were injured."

Sheriff Allen shook his head. "It concerns you, anyway, Miss Wilson, so I might as well ask you. It would be helpful if you remember anything about your accident. Has anything came back to you?"

When Anna admitted nothing had come back to her, Sheriff Allen sat with a humph next to Luke. "Something crazy is going on at the Weavers. One of the boys the Weavers had in their care, Noah, snuck out of the Weaver house in the middle of the night and went three miles to the Carson farm. He must have run the whole way in order to make it before Weaver realized he was gone. He said his brother has been missing for two days. He's scared Weaver did something to the boy. Jack's his name. The younger brother, Noah, has bruises on his face and arms. He said Weaver hits him whenever he doesn't do what he tells him."

A pain shot through Anna's neck and up through her head. She tried to massage it out.

"What's wrong?" Luke asked Anna.

"I think I may have just remembered something. The day I went to the Weavers to check on Jack and Noah, there was a loud noise before the horses bolted, and the buggy struck something." Anna closed her eyes.

"Do you remember anything else?" Sheriff Allen asked.

Anna looked up at the sheriff. "I wish I did."

"I'll have to take you to the Carson farm, since you are the representative for the orphanage which left the boys in the care of the Weavers. I'm hearing a story from Weaver I'm not inclined to believe. He says Jack

must have ran away when Noah did because they were
both in their beds last night when he checked on them.
He's convinced Noah lies to get attention, and his
bruises are from Jack and him fighting. It's Weaver's
word against Noah's. The only way to figure out this
mess is to find Jack. He's the key to the truth." Sheriff
Allen stood up.

"I'll do anything I can to help, Sheriff." Anna
followed Luke and Sheriff Allen down the steps.

"I left two deputies with Weaver and ordered them
to not let him out of their sight. That leaves me
shorthanded to conduct a good search. Luke, can you
spare any men to look for the boy?" Sheriff Allen
asked. "I understand you're fixing things, but if we're
going to find the boy alive, we need as many people
searching as possible."

Luke shouted at Ben who was walking out of the
barn. "Saddle Daisy for Miss Wilson! Also, tell Colt
and Steven to ride out with Miss Wilson and Sheriff
Allen to search for a missing boy."

Ben disappeared back into the barn.

Luke looked from Anna to the sheriff. "I can't leave
the ranch until Mr. Brown gets back, but I'll saddle up
the minute he returns. I hope Jack's okay." Luke
glanced at the sheriff. "You don't believe Weaver, do
you?"

"Never have. Unfortunately, I can't go off hunches.
I need evidence." Sheriff Allen untied his horse from
the hitching post.

"I've heard rumors about how bad he is when he
gets drunk, always trying to fight everyone around him.
He never fights fair either, does whatever he can to
win." Luke looked at Anna "Do you think the loud

noise Miss Wilson remembered was a gunshot?"

Sheriff Allen spit into the dirt. "Maybe. Maybe Miss Wilson saw something he didn't want her to. When she lost her memory from the fall, he must've felt relieved."

"What's his wife got to say?" Luke asked.

"She ain't around," said the sheriff. "Weaver says she's staying with her sister in town. I'll check that story out as soon as I have time."

Ben led two saddled horses. He gave Anna, Daisy's reins. Ben mounted his horse. Colt and Steven sat atop their horses near the gate. With no hay bale to use as a mounting block, Anna struggled to get her foot in Daisy's stirrup. Luke touched her shoulder and linked his hands together to boost her up. Luke reminded her to be careful or Mr. Brown wouldn't be happy he let her go with Sheriff Allen. Anna doubted if Joshua cared.

~

Anna settled herself at the Carson's kitchen table with Noah while the sheriff and Mr. Carson rode off in search of Jack. Beth Carson spooned heaping portions of beans and ham into Noah's bowl, but he only managed a couple of bites. Anna pushed her bowl away.

The Carson's farm was a tidy place with a freshly painted barn and a yard full of plump chickens. Mr. Carson had introduced her to a hired hand who had asked to ride with the search party. Anna saw no evidence of children on the farm.

Anna, Noah and Beth sat around the table in the cozy kitchen. Yellow curtains embroidered with tiny red flowers hung in the window. Beth was as cheerful as the choice of colors for her house. You couldn't help but be encouraged just being around her. She even managed to get Noah to smile.

"I can't wait until the men get back, Noah, so you can see Jack. Waiting is never an easy thing to do." Beth sat a plate of warm cookies in front of him.

Tears trickled down Noah's cheeks before he could wipe them away. "We should have run away when Jack wanted to. He knew right away that Mr. Weaver wasn't right."

"I'm sorry, Noah, that things turned out so hard for you and your brother. Those are good men looking for him now, and they won't come back without him, I'm certain of it. And, of course, I'm praying for Jack." Beth poured Noah a cup of milk. "Would you like milk or coffee, Miss Wilson?"

"Please call me Anna. A cup of coffee sounds good if it's not too much trouble." Anna scooted her chair closer to Noah and put her arm around his shoulders. "You'll never go back to the Weaver farm again, and when they find Jack, he won't either. I'm sorry you went through so much. The way you were treated was wrong."

"I remember the day you came, Miss Wilson. We wanted to leave with you, but Mr. Weaver made sure we couldn't. And right after you left, Mr. Weaver saddled his horse and rode off after you. I got a sick feeling in my stomach when he returned. He was happy and said we'd never see you again. I was afraid he hurt you. I'm glad you're okay." Noah gave Anna a timid smile.

"I'm sorry I didn't get back out to the farm to check on you again." Anna sat back in her chair.

"I'm glad you didn't, Miss Wilson. He would've

hurt you worse. He hurts everyone."

Horses thundered into the farm yard. Beth looked between the curtains before opening the door. Sheriff Allen and Bill Carson walked in.

The sheriff spoke to Noah. "We found your brother, son. Joshua felt it best if we got him as far from the Weaver place as possible, and I agree. He's taking Jack to his place. Ben went for the doctor. You and Miss Wilson will come with me to the Brown ranch. I'm glad we found Jack but you should know that Weaver got away from my deputies He's out there somewhere."

"Your brother has had a bad time of it. We found him tied to a tree and beat pretty bad. Weaver left him there to die. I want you to know something. I will not rest until Weaver is behind bars. He won't be hurting you or your brother ever again." Sheriff Allen looked at everyone in the room. "Let's get going."

Beth wrapped the cookies in a towel and pressed them into Noah's hands. She hugged him tightly. Anna admired her ability to love so easily.

Anna struggled to get her foot in the stirrup and finally managed to pull herself up into the saddle. She thought of how easy it had been to let Luke help her earlier. Mr. Carson lifted Noah up in front of Sheriff Allen. "Thank you." Anna said. "You both have helped so much." Bill wrapped his arm around Beth protectively as they all took off.

~

When they rode into the ranch, Anna saw Doc Fisher's horse tied in front of the house. Anna dismounted and hobbled up the steps. She wasn't used to all this riding. Sheriff Allen helped Noah down and he ran up the porch steps. Joshua met him at the front door and stopped him with a hand to his chest.

"Slow down, son."

"I need to see Jack." Noah pleaded. "Please let me go, mister."

Joshua asked Noah to join him on the porch so he could talk to him about Jack. Anna leaned against the railing, wondering if Joshua had bad news to break to Noah. Joshua explained to Noah that the doctor needed time to tend Jack's wounds. Once the doctor finished, Noah could go back and see his brother.

Noah's body trembled, and sobs burst from him. "I need my brother. He's all I have."

Anna pulled Noah into her arms.

Joshua stepped closer. "We'll do everything we can to help Jack get better. No matter what happens, you and Jack aren't alone. Miss Wilson is here for you, and I'll do whatever I can." Joshua waited for Noah to settle down. When he did, he offered Noah a rocking chair. He put his hand on the boy's knee. "We can pray for Jack if you'd like to?"

"I ain't talked to God much, and I'm not sure I want to. He hasn't cared about Jack and me." Noah looked at Joshua.

"I understand why it didn't feel like He cared for you and your brother when you were going through so many difficult things. This world can be a tough place to live. No one knows that better than Jesus. He suffered too so we could have a forever home. His heart's been breaking for both of you." Joshua cleared his throat.

Tears trickled down Anna's cheeks. If nothing else happened during her time in Texas, she was grateful to witness how Joshua cared for those around him. Noah wasn't a part of his life, yet he treated him like a son. The prayer comforted Noah, and it comforted Anna.

Joshua stood up and patted Noah's shoulder. "I happen to know there are some new puppies in the barn. There's also a new colt. Miss Wilson gave him quite the special name, Tornado."

"That's a great name. Noah wiped his tears away.

"The doctor will be with Jack for a while. By the time you've met Tornado and the puppies, I'm sure you'll be able to see him." Joshua glanced at Anna and smiled. The smile looked a little strained but Anna could see there was hope mixed in too.

Anna found Ella in the kitchen, spreading jam on bread for the children. "You make a wonderful big sister. They're lucky to have you here. I'm going to check on Jack, and then I can take over for you."

Ella poured water into Rebecca's cup. "Take your time. I promised to push the children on the swing and then we were going to play a game of tag."

Jack lay on the bed in the guest room. His face was swollen and bruised. She couldn't even see where one eye should be. Most troubling was that he wasn't moving, even though Doc Fisher was stitching a cut on his hand. Clara kept everything clean while he worked.

"How is he?" Anna asked.

Doc Fisher looked up from his work to see who he was talking to and bent right back to it. "To be honest, I'm not sure. He's been in and out of consciousness since I've been here."

Anna stepped closer. "That man is a beast."

Clara spoke quietly. "His pulse was weak when Doc Fisher got here but it's gotten better." She spooned water into Jack's mouth. "Besides the cuts, he has broken ribs, a goose egg on the back of his head, and his shoulder has been dislocated. Doc Fisher wrapped his ribs and stitched the deeper cuts. He still had to set his shoulder."

Anna stood at the head of the bed and gently moved a few strands of hair back from Jack's forehead. "How anybody can treat someone like this I will never understand."

"Weaver treats everyone anyway he wants, because he feels justified in what he does." Doc Fisher wiped his forehead with his sleeve. "Mrs. Brown, can you open the window?"

Clara lifted the sash and rubbed her injured arm.

The doctor noted Clara's discomfort. "Mrs. Brown, if you need a break, Anna can help me."

"I should have offered earlier." Anna patted her shoulder. "Why don't you rest?"

Anna took over spooning water into Jack's mouth. Clara excused herself to check the children and to make coffee. She promised to sit down in the kitchen for a bit.

The doctor put a knee to Jack's shoulder and took hold of his arm with both hands. "You might want to avert your gaze for a minute." No sooner had Anna looked away than she heard the doctor straining. The arm snapped back in place and she felt sick to her stomach.

Doc Fisher laid Noah's arm across his stomach. "All right, it's in place. I have a roll of cloth strips in my bag and some large pieces of cotton. Can you get those for me, Miss Wilson?"

Anna handed him the supplies. "Do you need anything else?"

"Would you help me wrap the wound on his head? If you could hold him on his good side that would be a great help." Dr. Fisher wound the cloth strips around his head. When he finished, he cut the end of the strips and tied them into place. "I'm going to see if Mrs. Brown has the coffee ready. I've done all I can for now."

"I'll see he gets more water." Anna sat in the chair.

She watched Doc Fisher leave the room, then laid her head back and closed her eyes. The instant she did, regret sickened her. She shouldn't have waited so long to check on the Weaver farm again. Anna rolled her knotted shoulders and picked up the spoon.

A light tap sounded on the door. It was Noah.

He inched forward, his eyes never leaving his brother's face. "He looks awful bad."

"Doc Fisher is a good doctor. Jack has a real good chance of getting better." Anna patted the chair next to her and Noah sat down.

"Is it okay if I sleep in here on the floor?" Noah asked. "I want to be by Jack."

"I'll get blankets and make you a bed. One of us will always be in here too." Anna smiled at Noah.

Noah and Anna sat in silence until Doc Fisher returned. He wiped his hands on one of Clara's tea towels. "That's about all I can do for the boy tonight. I'll be back in the morning. I've left something for the pain if he wakes up. Have a good night." Doc Fisher snapped his bag closed and left. Clara and Joshua came into the room a few minutes later.

"You look tired, Anna. Why don't I take the first watch? You can get some rest and come back around two." Joshua walked over by Noah.

Anna was grateful for a chance to close her eyes. "Let me get Noah some blankets." Anna walked past Joshua without looking up. "I can get the blankets, Anna, go ahead and go to bed." Clara followed her out the door.

Anna laid down and pulled the quilt up. She couldn't get her brain to stop spinning. She would telegraph the orphanage and explain what happened to the boys. Anna wondered if there would be any chance of finding another family for Jack and Noah here. She didn't want to take them back to the orphanage. She didn't want to take Ella back either.

As muddled as she was, she even wondered if Bennett was the best course. He had proclaimed his love for her. She doubted he would welcome one, possibly three more children that Anna intended to keep by her side.

Just before sleep claimed her, she determined to get Jack better before making any plans, but those plans would include a loving home for him and Noah.

Chapter Twelve

Joshua watched Doc Fisher heft himself into his saddle. Although he wanted to hear good news about Jack, Doc Fisher was concerned.

"He won't stay awake more than a few minutes at a time. That could mean brain damage, and only time will give us a complete picture of the extent of what happened. The swelling in his face is going down, but the bruising is getting darker. Weaver didn't take it easy when he hit Jack." Doc Fisher looked toward the west where a curtain of rain swept the far horizon. "I'll be back again tomorrow. You can send one of your men if there are any troubling changes." The doctor reined his horse toward the road and urged his tired mare into a trot.

Inside the house, Noah sat in the bedroom waiting for his brother to wake up, crying off and on. Anna kept her head bent as if the weight of everything that had happened was on her. He wanted to talk to her but didn't know how to approach her after their conversation had ended so badly the other night. Some of his men were trying to break one of their newer horses. This was just the distraction Joshua needed from the sadness engulfing the house.

Still, he worried Weaver might return to cause trouble, so he'd posted a couple of men to watch over the ranch day and night. If Weaver showed up, they were to shoot if he made any hesitation in doing what they asked.

"Hey boss, how's the boy?" Jim called as Joshua neared the corral.

"No change."

"Too bad. We're wanting that young man to pull through. Can't believe someone like Weaver is still alive, he shouldn't be." Jim pushed his cowboy hat back on his forehead.

"He won't last long if he gives the men on watch any trouble. I don't want anyone else hurt because of him." Joshua watched a second guy get thrown from the black stallion.

"As far as I'm concerned, Weaver lost his rights when he hurt that boy." Jim spit a long stream of tobacco in the dirt. "We're heading out to the upper pasture we didn't make it to yesterday. I hope our luck continues with the cattle today, looks like the tornado missed them all. We'll be back before nightfall."

Thinking the boy could use a break from watching his brother, Joshua walked toward the house to get Noah. The puppies seemed to distract him from his burdens the day before.

The day was beautiful, not a cloud anywhere. It was hard to recall the violence of the tornado, especially now that the repairs were all but done. Joshua was thankful the tornado hadn't made a direct hit on the ranch. Just as he opened the front door, Anna stood from the swing.

Joshua walked over and sat in his favorite rocking chair. "I hope you're not leaving. Can we talk?"

Anna sat back down and pushed the porch swing with her foot. "I've made some decisions I need to talk to you about. As soon as Jack is able to travel, we'll be leaving. I have another family to visit and then I will be done. Thank you for helping us so much. I agreed to stay here to help you and Clara, but I brought more problems than help, I'm afraid.

"I won't take Seth or Rebecca from you Joshua. I've learned from being here that you'll do whatever's needed to make sure everyone's taken care of. You do need to find one more woman to help Clara if not two. The ranch requires a lot from Clara. Not only does she have the children to take care of, but there are the house and garden." Anna picked one of the small roses from the climbing bush beside her and smelled it.

"There have been inquiries to the ads I placed. Two women will be out to the ranch sometime this week to talk with me. I hope you know that there's no need for you and Ella and the boys to rush leaving or even to leave at all. You're welcome to stay as long as you want." Joshua looked over at the oak tree, the children's swing was moving in the breeze ever so slightly. Birds flew in and around the branches, tweeting their happy songs. *If only my life could be so carefree.*

"The longer we stay here, the harder it will be for us to leave. I want to find a way to keep Ella with me, and if at all possible Noah and Jack too. I'm thinking of getting my teaching certificate and then looking for a job out west. Working as an orphan train agent isn't for

Darlia Sawyer

me. I don't feel placing children with families where they are beaten or worse is the best answer. There are good families too but is it worth the risk?" Anna looked at Joshua.

"If they stayed in New York City, Anna, would they have even had a chance at a better life? They probably would've starved, frozen, or died from disease. By bringing them out west and finding families for them, you gave them a chance. Yes, there are evil people, but the majority aren't." Joshua got up and sat next to her on the swing. "I know you don't believe this, but God loves them, and He doesn't want them to be hurt. He lets each of us make our own choices which allows some people to make wrong choices which hurt our loved ones. One day they'll answer for those choices, Anna. I know it doesn't feel fair, and it isn't, but it's the price we pay for freedom." Joshua longed to take Anna in his arms. He always felt that way when he was near enough to get lost in the warmth of her gaze or the smell of lilac soap on her skin.

"I know you love, God, Joshua. If He really loved everyone as much as you say He does wouldn't He keep bad things from happening? God doesn't really care." Anna looked over at the barn. "It's better if I leave. I can't accept a God who allows so much pain."

The rattle of a wagon drew Joshua's attention. The Carson's drove up the lane. In all the years he'd lived on the ranch, the Carson's had never visited before.

"Hey, Joshua." Bill Carson jumped down from the wagon seat and helped his wife down. "We wanted to check on the boys. How are they doing?"

"Noah hasn't left his brother's bedside except to eat and to visit some new puppies. Jack is in and out of consciousness, which worries the doctor the most. All of his other injuries are healing." Joshua patted Bill on the back as he walked by. "It's awfully good to see you folks. Make yourselves comfortable."

Beth sat by Anna on the porch swing and hugged her. "You must be exhausted."

"I can get rest once Jack is on the mend." Anna stood up. "It's my turn to sit with him. Would you like to go in with me?"

Beth stood back up. "Obviously, I can't decide if I'm sitting or standing." She giggled.

"If you'd like to see him, Mr. Carson, come in when you're ready." Anna and Beth went into the house.

~

Joshua was in the barn doing what he did best when he needed to think, cleaning stalls. He'd done this chore since he could barely lift a shovel or pitch fork. Joshua actually liked the smell of manure and horse sweat. He wouldn't trade what he did every day for any other job he could think of. Some people might think it the worst job you could do, but he loved pretty much every aspect of operating a ranch.

It turned out that Bill and Beth had come to the ranch with a plan to present to Anna. They wanted to bring Jack and Noah into their home. Bill had been abused by his father so he knew how awful it could be. He wanted to help the boys deal with all the thoughts and feelings they might have after being in such a bad home.

The Carson's had given their offer a lot of thought. If being in their home didn't work out for the boys or for them, they'd take them back to the orphanage in New York City. They wanted everyone to be happy.

Bill felt God had guided Noah to their door. They had been praying for a child, but it didn't look like they could have any of their own.

Anna promised to talk to the boys once Jack was better. She appreciated the Carson's offer. Bill and Beth asked Anna if they could come out and see the boys every couple of days. Anna agreed it would be a great idea.

Ella ran through the barn doors. "Mr. Brown. Jack has been awake for ten whole minutes. You have to come and see."

"That is the best news I've heard all day." Joshua jabbed his pitch fork into a pile of hay. "I'm excited to talk with him. I bet Noah was jumping up and down."

Joshua watched Ella's red curls bounce as she raced in front of him. He would miss Ella when she and Anna left. His mother adored her, and she was a huge help to everyone. Her smile could chase away all the sad things in a day. She'd surely worked her way into Joshua's heart. He would offer her a home here even if Anna left, but he knew Ella would not leave Anna.

Jack's eyes were open, and he was trying to smile, but the swelling made it look lopsided. His bruises had faded to a ghastly yellowish green.

"It looks like we need to send someone to get Doc Fisher? He'll be very happy to see you staying awake." The boy watched Joshua with wary eyes, so Joshua stayed in the doorway. He couldn't blame the boy for being cautious after all he'd been through.

Clara propped Jack up with extra pillows. "Seth went to tell Luke, so I'm guessing Ben is already on his way to the doctor's."

"How are you feeling, Jack?" Joshua asked.

"I have a bad headache, and it feels like every part of my body is hurting."

"You've been through a lot, son, and it's going to take your body time to heal. Doc Fisher left some medicine for the pain. We've been praying for you." Joshua glanced at Anna. She had dark circles under her eyes and could barely keep them open. "My mother and Miss Wilson have been taking good care of you."

Jack thanked all of them for finding and helping him. Clara gave him a cup of water and promised him chicken and dumplings and deep dish apple pie for supper if the doctor said it was all right. Jack did manage to smile big for that despite the swelling.

~

Joshua sat in the rocking chair on the front porch trying to relax before he made his way to the noisy bunk house and the hard mattress. It had been a long day. There wasn't a hint of a breeze and his shirt stuck to his back. Stars twinkled in every direction. Normally, star gazing distracted him, but his mind was whirling from one subject to another.

Saying prayers with the children had helped calm Joshua. Although, when he thought about his children and how they could've ended up in a home like Jack and Noah, it made him sick to his stomach. He'd always treated and loved Seth and Rebecca the same as he did Emily.

Animals like Weaver deserved to be hunted down, taken to jail, given a trial and hung. He didn't feel comfortable with those feelings, but they were honest.

The doctor still worried the beating had damaged Jack's brain. When he talked, it was hard for him to get all the words out he was trying to say. Some doctors in

117

the east were suggesting that the brain swelled with trauma and could heal over time. That was Jack's best hope.

Ben not only brought the doctor, he brought Sheriff Allen, who was anxious to talk to Jack. Joshua couldn't believe the things Jack told the sheriff. Noah hadn't talked much about what happened at the Weavers, and they hadn't wanted to press him because he was worried about Jack. Joshua watched Anna as Jack relayed what life had been like for him and Noah at the Weavers. He knew she was heaping guilt upon herself for not getting the boys out of that situation. After Jack finished, she left the room and went upstairs.

The sheriff opened the front door. "That pie was delicious but it's going to be a long ride back to town. I'm so full I can hardly walk."

"Miss Wilson does make great pie. Are you getting close to finding Weaver?" Joshua stood up and followed the sheriff down the steps.

"It's like he's vanished."

"What about his wife? Is she helping?" Joshua pressed.

"She's happy to be with her sister. As far as she's concerned, she hopes to never lay eyes on him again. He almost killed her a couple times. She would be happy to see him locked up. There's a deputy watching the sister's home, but I don't hold out much hope of ever seeing that sorry excuse for a man anytime soon."

"What about that sister, hadn't she ever suspected something was going on?"

"According to the sister, Mrs. Weaver always had a reason for her bruises." The sheriff toed at the dirt with his boot. "I can't arrest a man on rumors. Wish I could.

The wife needed to make a complaint."

Joshua leaned in. "Sheriff, do we have any reason to fear Weaver?"

"The wife told me Weaver had hoped to kill Miss Wilson that day. Not to mention you have the two boys who are a reminder to him that they got away. He sees that as a personal insult to his manhood. You're wise to keep guards posted. I'll keep looking for him, but I wouldn't underestimate his need for revenge."

Joshua watched the sheriff ride off. He felt a chill go down his back. Was Weaver watching the ranch, waiting for the moment he could catch them off guard. He needed to talk with his men, under no circumstance was anyone to leave the ranch alone. Nor should there ever be a time someone wasn't keeping guard. A lot was at stake and he wasn't willing to let Weaver claim any more victims.

Chapter Thirteen

In the three weeks since Jack was found, his wounds had healed. Anna helping him daily with his speech. It was apparent that the blows to his head had affected his ability to talk. Despite the frustration of halting and unclear speech, he was making slow progress.

As they had promised, Bill and Beth Carson came to the ranch every couple of days to visit the boys. They told Noah and Jack they'd like them to live at their farm. The boys were hesitant at first, but as they got to know the couple better they liked the idea of living with them. Anna wondered if they feared Weaver would return for them. No one had seen or heard from him in such a long time that she no longer startled at every sudden noise. Although, she still felt guilty because she hadn't gone to check on the boys in time to save Jack from getting hurt. Knowing Jack and Noah would have such a great family helped Anna feel a bit better about being an agent on the orphan trains.

~

The girls were down for their naps and the ranch

house was quiet. Noah, Jack and Seth were with Luke in the barn. The boys loved being around the animals and helping Luke feed and take care of them. They each had picked out a favorite puppy and Anna hoped the Carson's would be okay with two new dogs along with two new boys.

Anna sat on the porch swing where she waited for Ben to hitch the horses to a wagon. It was time to move toward her future. That meant a trip to Nacogdoches to buy train tickets to New York City. Her heart rebelled at buying the train tickets, but she knew she couldn't stay on the ranch much longer.

She would miss the rhythms and peace of the ranch. Anna had lived her life among the hustle and bustle of New York City, but time didn't hold the same meaning in Texas. The days still passed quickly, but there was time to rest and enjoy the star filled sky at night and to sit by a lake having a picnic. The flowers smelled sweeter in Texas, and the air was definitely cleaner.

She couldn't let herself dwell on what she would miss. She planned out her day in town. First, she would buy special treats to surprise the children. This was her way of saying she loved them and saying she was sorry. The clip clopping of horse hoofs on the packed dirt woke Anna from her daydreams. Ben drove the wagon and Luke walked beside him.

Why is Luke with Ben?

"You weren't planning on going alone, were you?" Luke's tone reminded her of her father's when he thought she was about to do something she shouldn't.

She stood and straightened her skirt. "I am, it's only a two hour trip, so I'll be back in plenty of time to help Clara make dinner." Anna climbed into the wagon and took the reins from Ben. "I'm fully capable of driving myself."

Luke grabbed the horse's reins. "I don't think so. You can't go by yourself. I promised Mr. Brown no one would leave this ranch alone. Ben will go with you."

"I'm not going to take off, you didn't have to hold the reins." Anna smiled.

"I am never sure with you Miss Wilson, you just might." Luke laughed. "Besides, we both know this has nothing to do with your ability to drive a wagon or any plans you may have to take off. Weaver is still out there somewhere. Going anywhere unattended is unwise, Ma'am."

Ben opened his hands for the reins.

Anna reluctantly handed them over. "Weaver would be a fool to hang around Nacogdoches. The whole county knows what he's done, and there is a price on his head." Anna sat back with a huff.

"We would all feel better if you had someone with you who can handle a gun, Anna." Luke swatted a fly buzzing around his head.

Anna couldn't argue with their concern, but she didn't like how superior they sounded. "Men. You're all the same, bossy and overprotective. I obviously have no say in this but I don't have to like it." Anna tied her bonnet strings as Ben turned the horses and headed toward the gate. Luke chuckled behind them.

"I'm sorry you have to babysit me, Ben. I'm sure you had better things to do."

Ben turned toward her and smiled. "I don't mind, Miss Wilson. I can't think of anything better to do than driving a pretty woman to town. I feel kind of sorry for everyone on the ranch."

"Well, thank you but I feel bad you had to give up what you were doing." Anna smiled.

"What do you plan on doing in town?"

Anna tucked her purse under the bench. "I have train tickets to buy, and I want to get a surprise for the children. It shouldn't take long."

Ben pushed his hat back on his forehead. "Train tickets for who? You aren't planning on leaving, are you?"

The road followed the shoreline of a small lake. The water shimmered in the sun's rays as a slight breeze ruffled the leaves of the surrounding trees. "Ella and I will be heading back to New York City in a couple of weeks. I've stayed longer than I'd planned, and it's time we go home. We'll miss being here with all of you, far more than you'll ever know."

"I thought you'd be staying here. How is Mrs. Brown going to do everything without your help?" Ben lightly flipped the reins to get the horses moving faster.

"Mr. Brown has talked to a couple of women who will be moving out to the ranch soon to help." Anna felt a little jealous, knowing she wouldn't be the one there helping.

The horses kicked up a cloud of dust, and Ben cleared his throat. "It won't be the same without you and Miss Ella around. We'll all miss the two of you."

A movement caught the corner of Anna's eye as a loud explosion rang out. Liquid droplets hit her in the face, and Ben slumped onto her lap. His blood seeped into her skirt. Anna fumbled with the reins in Ben's hands. The weight of his body pressed down on her. She couldn't heft him aside to get a good grip.

Behind them, a horse galloped closer and closer.

She reached toward Ben's waist, feeling for his gun. The horses were slowing down. She had the gun half way out but still couldn't reach the reins. The rider was astride the wagon. A bandana covered most of his face.

"Put your hands in the air." The man held his gun pointed at her.

Anna had to let go of the gun even though it was her only defense and put her hands up. "Why did you shoot him? We don't have any money. Let us go! I need to get him to a doctor."

"Shut up! You're going with me. We have a debt to settle." The man's voice sounded familiar.

"Weaver?" Anna felt panic like she'd never known before grip her insides with giant talons. She knew he would kill her. "I'm not going with you."

"If you don't, I'll make sure your friend's dead. Get down from the wagon." Weaver kept the gun pointed on Ben. "Now!"

Anna laid Ben's head on the bench as she scooted herself out from under him. She slowly got off the wagon. Her brain was racing through multiple scenarios on how she could get out of this, but they all ended at the same thought, she couldn't refuse him. The only hope she had was in someone hearing the gun shot.

"Get over here or I put another bullet in him." Weaver cocked the gun.

Trembling, Anna walked toward his horse. "Let me stop his bleeding."

"Quiet!" Weaver reached down, grabbed her arm and pulled her onto the horse across his lap. Weaver kicked his horse in the side, the horse lurched into a gallop.

Weaver grasped hold of her dress. Even so, with

each jolt from the horse's gait, Anna's legs dangled and flopped up and down. She felt as if she would fall off. If she fell off, maybe she could escape. She had to try.

She elbowed Weaver in the groin. He cussed and jerked back in pain. Anna fell off the horse, hitting the ground hard. She tried sucking in air, but couldn't. She struggled to get up. Weaver pulled back on his horse and was bent over. Anna pulled up her skirt and ran. *Why didn't I bring a gun?* She should have listened to Joshua. A rope fell over her body, tightened and dragged her toward Weaver's horse. He dismounted and yanked her up against him. He grabbed her hair, pulled her head back and ground his mouth into her lips. Anna bit him and he slapped her across the face.

Weaver roughly took the lasso off from around her. "I promise you will pay for that little escape. Get in the saddle before I go back and finish off that man."

Anna put her foot in the stirrup and managed to get in the saddle. Weaver mounted the horse behind her. "Try that again, and you'll breathe your last. Once I have a little fun with you, I'm leaving this town. I just couldn't leave without thankn' you for messing up my life. If you hadn't come here, I'd still have my farm and my wife." Weaver spat out.

"You can't blame me for your troubles. You messed up your own life by hurting the people around you. What kind of monster are you?" Anna tried to pry his fingers off her. He gripped her tighter, making her stomach hurt. Her face burned where he'd slapped her, and she could taste blood from her cut lip.

"Those boys were treated better than my father done treated me and I turned out good enough. You have to teach people respect, just like I'm gonna teach you."

Weaver laughed in her ear.

"Beating someone is not how you teach respect." Anna was dying on the inside, hope was in a place she could no longer feel.

"My father showed me plenty of love at the end of his fist. If your family won't listen to you, you ain't got nothin'. Those boys had food, clothes and shelter. What did I get? No farm and no wife." Weaver spat into the dirt.

"You left Jack for dead. A dead child doesn't respect anyone." Anna hated this man with all that was in her.

"I was gonna fetch him after a day or so, but then that brat brother of his ran off and sent the sheriff. They got them kids under constant watch, or I would make sure he learned his lesson. They shoulda done better with you. I'm done talking." He kicked the horse over and over in its side. They raced across fields of waist high grass.

The wind whipped Anna's hair into her face. Tears ran down her cheeks. *He's going to kill me.*

What could she do or say to make this man let her go?

She hoped Joshua found Ben in time.

I have no one.

Chapter Fourteen

Joshua rode into the ranch early with his men. He was looking forward to time with the children. He was rubbing down his horse when Luke informed him Ben and Anna had gone to town and should be back soon. Joshua lifted Midnight's foot to clean his hoof. He shook his head. Anna could be impatient. He wasn't comfortable with anyone leaving the ranch without a few men with them. Weaver was still out there somewhere.

Joshua guessed she was buying train tickets. He'd overheard her talking to his mother. Clara had tried to change Anna's mind, but she insisted leaving was for the best. Joshua didn't want to say goodbye. He wasn't ready for them to leave.

The clomp of hooves and the rattle of a wagon told him he'd worried about nothing. Anna and Ben had arrived back safely. He led Midnight into a stall and watched the horse nuzzle his feed.

Why had Anna been dropped into their lives? She came at a time he desperately needed help for his mother. Although, with her accident and Jack's injuries the workload had increased, at times, for everyone too. It hadn't been Anna's fault those things happened, and he was glad her and Ella hadn't been alone during those times. Ella had been a life saver through it all. No matter the reason Anna and Ella were here, it wouldn't help the goodbyes hurt any less.

Anna and Ella fit into the ranch as if they'd always been there. He cared way too much for Anna, way beyond where he said he'd ever allow his heart to go again. Would God direct her to his ranch when there could never be a future for them?

"Hey boss," Luke called to Joshua. "You better get out here. It's Doc Fisher in our wagon."

Joshua walked out of the barn with a sinking heart. *What now?* Dr. Fisher drove the wagon grim-faced with his horse tied behind. His men seemed to sense the wrongness of the scene and rushed from the barn, the corral, and bunkhouse. Soon they were gingerly lifting Ben out of the wagon bed.

Ice cold fingers of dread gripped Joshua's heart. "Where's Anna? What happened to Ben?"

Doc Fisher climbed down from his seat, carrying his bag. Surprise lifted his haggard face. "I have no idea where Miss Wilson is. I found Ben and the wagon in the middle of the road closer to town." The doctor directed the men toward the house. "I was headed to the Taylor farm when I saw the wagon and Ben slumped over. I got the bleeding stopped and headed here. There's a purse under the wagon bench, so it must not have been a robbery."

Luke sent Jake to saddle a horse and ride for Sheriff Allen.

Once Ben was situated, Joshua turned to his men standing outside the bedroom door, nervously watching the doctor tend their friend's wound. "We can't do anything more for Ben just now, but he's in good hands. We're heading out to find Miss Wilson. I need four men with a fresh mount and a sidearm." Joshua turned to Luke. "Jim can watch the ranch. You're with me. Anna trusts you, and I hope you can help me figure out where she is."

"We'll be ready to ride in a few minutes." Luke walked out the door.

Clara came into the room. "What happened?"

"Ben's been shot. We don't know where Anna is. Please be praying, Mother. I don't like the way this looks." Luke gave his mother a hug and went out the door.

"I'll be praying and I'll explain things to the children. Be careful. My guess would be Henry Weaver's involved in this." Clara followed Joshua down the hall.

Joshua slapped his hat against his leg. "It has to be him. Anna's purse was left in the wagon, so it wasn't a robbery. If at all possible, I'll bring Anna back here alive. I won't let him hurt anyone else. He has to be stopped."

Clara stepped closer. "This is the sheriff's work, son."

"I'm not waiting for the sheriff." Joshua bounded down the steps and mounted his horse. Luke and four other men joined him.

"I can get more men if you think we need them." Luke said.

"I think we're fine. I'm pretty sure Weaver has her.

There's only one of him, so I trust we can take him down with six of us." Joshua spurred his horse. "Let's go!"

~

"This is the place Doc Fisher said he came across the wagon." Joshua got down to look for clues. The deep dust had been trampled. He couldn't make out one horse print from another.

Luke rose from where he studied the ground. "Hey boss, a lone horse went off in that direction. And I'd guess there were two people on him by how deep the prints sunk in the dirt." Luke got back up on his horse. "Looks like he has Anna."

They'd gone a short distance when they found a spot where the horse stopped. Luke got off his horse for a closer look. "It looks like someone was dragged, and then there might have been a scuffle here. The horse takes off again to the east." Luke glanced at Joshua.

"I swear, if that man hurts her, he will pay." Heat surged through Joshua's body and hatred and anger consumed him.

Vengeance is mine, Joshua.

Joshua understood that to be true, but right now anger was burning inside him and he had no wish to listen. He spurred his horse and gave him his head. They had time to make up and it was starting to rain.

Chapter Fifteen

Rain soaked Anna's clothes. Her whole body ached from falling off the horse. Her face and lips throbbed. Blood had crusted on her lips.

Hate for Weaver consumed her. Escaping seemed impossible, but she remained alert to every possibility. *I wonder if they found Ben and are looking for me.* If so, her only hope was to be found quickly. Large drops fell from the trees in the unfamiliar forest as Weaver urged the horse over fallen logs.

The trees thinned as they started up a rocky trail. "Whoa." Weaver pulled back on the reins. Drenched from the rain, a breeze sent a chill to the very core of Anna's being. She wanted to get out of the rain, but she definitely didn't want to stop. Her only hope was for them to keep moving. She tried to keep thoughts of what Weaver might do to her in the back of her mind. Anna couldn't let fear overcome her as she needed to think clearly. Thinking clearly was the only weapon she had.

Weaver pushed Anna from the horse. She landed

hard on her injured ankle. The pain shot through her leg as she suppressed a gasp. Weaver pointed up the side of the hill. She saw what appeared to be a cave, but shrubs obstructed the view.

Weaver shoved her again. "Get up there and into that cave."

Anna looked back at the way they'd come. The forest lay dark, deep, and silent.

"I said, get in the cave!" Weaver kicked her leg.

Anna hit the ground, small rocks digging into her palms. She managed to get up and put most of her weight on her left leg. She hobbled into the cave. The man was an animal. His anger fed off of her vulnerability. She straightened to her full height, but the cold and wet shook Anna. The hopelessness of her situation brought bile to her throat. She sank into the shadows as Weaver entered the cave. *I hope Joshua will keep Ella if I can't make it out from here alive.*

Weaver gathered sticks and leaves in the cave, and there was a small pile of branches in one corner. Anna had heard that whenever someone left a deserted cave or cabin, they left wood for the next person to use. She wasn't sure she appreciated their kindness. Weaver's presence in the cave was menacing.

"Trying to hide won't do ya no good. It's time someone showed you what happens to women who don't mind their own business. You had no right messin' up my life. Now, I have no farm or wife. Yep, you're sure gonna pay." Weaver shaved pieces of wood for kindling with his knife.

A rustling noise outside the cave drew Weaver's attention. He pulled his gun. "I woulda thought that bullet I put in that man done killed 'im. Don't know how he survived long enough to come to your rescue." Weaver hurried toward the mouth of cave. "I got my gun right here, so don't try anything stupid. You have nowhere to go." He sneaked out of the cave with his gun drawn.

Anna wondered what was worse, letting this filthy man touch her or getting shot. She had to keep her wits about her and find a way to stop him. Being aware of opportunities was her only chance of escape. Anna didn't know how she would get away because Weaver was big, she didn't have a weapon, and she was hurt.

A gleam of light reflected off something metal next to the fire. Weaver must have left his knife behind when he went to check on the noise. He stood with his back to her at the mouth of the cave. She quickly moved forward, knelt and grabbed the knife, slipping it into her stocking. The blade poked into her leg, but she couldn't let it bother her, it might be her only chance of escape. She edged back into the shadows.

Weaver led the horse inside the cave. He ate a biscuit from his saddlebag in two bites and drank deeply from his canteen. He drew his sleeve over his mouth. "Too bad I didn't bring any for you," he laughed. He tied the horse to a boulder, took out a blanket from his saddle bag and laid it on the ground. "Get over here now." Weaver sat on the blanket.

Anna stood frozen in place, her whole body trembling.

I can't do this. Jesus, help me. I need you. I'm so sorry. In that moment, Anna knew she was not alone. A warmth flowed through her and stopped her trembling.

"I said get over here." Weaver cocked his gun and pointed it at her.

Anna limped toward him. The point of the knife blade pierced her skin with each step. How could she get to the knife without him noticing? Weaver grabbed her arm and pulled her down beside him, then yanked her head back as he pulled her hair.

"You asked for this. If you'd a just minded your own business, I'd still be at my farm and you could'a lived happily ever after with that rancher man. Even if I let you live, he won't want you for his wife. You wouldn't be worthy of his high and mighty self. He pretty much thinks he's a preacher man." Weaver stared into Anna's eyes. "There's nothing you can do." Weaver chuckled and ground his mouth into Anna's.

Pain shot through her from the cuts on her lips. His hands groped her, but she had to disconnect herself from what he was doing and focus on getting the knife. Buttons popped and her dress ripped as her hand touched the handle. Weaver shoved her to the cave floor, and she lost all progress she had made at getting the knife. Disgusted and nauseous, she drew her leg up and stretched toward the knife's handle. She gripped the handle between her fingers and inched it out from her stocking. Weaver was too busy ripping her dress apart to notice.

All the hatred and anger within her erupted as she buried the knife into Weaver's neck with all her might. Weaver let out a gasp as he grabbed his neck. Anna pushed him away and scrambled to her feet. He grabbed at the hem of her dress but she pulled herself free. She limped to the horse as fast as she could and untied the reins. She heard a gun cock as she pulled herself up into the saddle. The gun went off, a burning pain sliced into her arm. The horse bolted into a gallop at the sound of the gunshot. Anna struggled to hang on. Another shot rang out. Anna braced herself for death but the bullet missed. Blood ran down her arm from the first bullet which had met its target. She felt light headed and wondered if she would pass out. The horse was running to nowhere, and she didn't care. She had to get away from Weaver.

Please help me, I don't want to die.

Chapter Sixteen

It was late afternoon when the horse tracks ended at a rocky trail leading up to a ledge. Joshua and his men dismounted and made their way quietly up to the overhang. The rocks were slippery after all the rain and hindered their climb.

Joshua inched into the cave with his gun drawn. Inside a man lay on a blanket. Joshua cocked his gun and stepped closer. Luke followed right behind. Joshua breathed a prayer of thanks that Anna wasn't in the cave. The man didn't move, but as he got closer; he heard labored breathing.

"Make a move, and you're dead." Joshua spoke to the back of the man.

"Don't matter to me. I'm dying anyway. Lost too much blood," the man whispered.

Luke pointed his gun at the man's back. "It's Weaver. Be careful boss, he's probably lying."

Weaver moaned in pain. "Well, if it ain't the high and mighty rancher man come to rescue his true love."

Joshua moved closer. "Where is she?"

"Wouldn't you like to know? I had my fun, guess you want yours." Weaver gurgled as he tried to laugh.

"Doesn't look like you had much fun to me." Joshua knelt beside Weaver and rolled him onto his back. Blood ran from his neck and saturated the blanket below him. "You're half dead and she must have done it."

"I got myself distracted by the lovely Miss Wilson's hidden treasures." Weaver sneered. "I'd hoped you'd find her raped, beaten and dead. The only thing she might not be is dead although I shot her twice as she rode outta here."

"You filthy pig! Hell won't be hot enough for the likes of you. It's a good thing I'm not your judge." Joshua fingered the trigger of his gun and lowered the hammer. It was up to God to decide when his life ended. His anger was replaced by something else, a desperation to find Anna. He had to find her. Luke could handle this piece of trash.

Joshua mounted his horse, barking orders for Steven to ride with him. He told the others to return to the ranch once Weaver died. "Leave him where he fell. The sheriff will handle him."

"Too bad you failed at keepin' your woman safe." Weaver tried to laugh.

Joshua made himself ride away.

~

Joshua and Steven made slow progress through the dense undergrowth of the forest. It rained off and on, making the ground so wet that some of the tracks became puddles. They found a few blood drops, so they knew one of Weaver's shots hit her. The sun was about to set. Joshua knew they'd have to stop, or they'd lose the tracks.

"You about ready to make camp, boss? Daylight's about burnt out." Steven pointed to a clearing up ahead. "Looks like a good spot."

"I don't want to stop, but you're right. If we don't, we'll waste time wandering around not knowing where to go and lose all chance of finding the tracks again. This is not what I'd hoped for." *Help me find her God.*

When they dismounted, Joshua heard a horse nicker in the distance. "Did you hear that?"

"I did. Do you want me to see what's there?"

"I'll nose around, see what I can find. It will be dark soon. Get a fire going."

Joshua pushed through the trees and undergrowth. He stopped to listen. The horse whinnied again, and it was close. He changed his course and walked faster. He found the horse standing over a woman, face down on the ground. He recognized the blue of Anna's dress. Joshua felt her neck for a pulse. It was faint but steady. *Thank you Jesus.* "Anna, can you hear me?"

No response.

Joshua turned her over. The front of her dress and undergarments were ripped to expose her bruised and muddy skin. He took off his slicker and covered her. He hefted her up and carried her back to camp. He found Steven struggling to build a fire in the wet grass.

"I found Miss Wilson. Go get the horse while I check her for injuries." Joshua didn't want Steven seeing her ripped clothing, but wasn't sure how he was going to keep her covered.

Joshua gently laid her next to the fire. Blood soaked the sleeve of her dress, so he slit the material up her arm with his knife. One bullet hole, but no exit wound.

The bullet must still be in there. There weren't any other bullet wounds, but he worried she might have broken bones. He did a quick examination but didn't notice anything abnormal. *Should I try to get her back to the ranch tonight?*

This area was foreign to him, but if he followed the creek, he should get to a place where he would know which way to go. Tearing off part of Anna's hem, Joshua wrapped the wound tightly to slow the bleeding, then pulled the slicker back around her and buttoned the front.

"Here's the horse, he looks wore out. I'll tie him to my saddle." Steven said.

"We need to get back to the ranch. Her pulse is weak, and I'm worried she'll lose too much blood if we wait out the night. I have it wrapped. We'll have to take it slow." Joshua mounted his horse. Steven lifted Anna and Joshua pulled her into his lap. She groaned with the strain but didn't wake. Joshua told Steven his plan about following the stream. "I'll hold her as still as possible. I don't want to start the bleeding again."

~

Joshua and Steven made it to the ranch around midnight. When they rode up, Luke was sitting in a rocking chair on the porch. Joshua marveled at how quickly he'd returned from the cave.

Luke caught Anna in his arms. "Hurry her inside, Luke. Steven, it's been a rough day, but I need you to ride hard for the doctor."

Luke turned back to the men. "The doctor just left about an hour ago. Ben didn't make it." Luke continued up the porch steps.

Joshua's heart sank as he followed Luke and Anna

into the house. His hatred for Weaver grew with each step. "I can't believe Ben's gone. He was such a great kid."

"Doc is taking Ben's body to town to prepare it for burial." Luke laid Anna on Clara's bed.

Clara hurried into the room. "Thank heavens you found her. You gentlemen need to turn around a moment while I check her." She opened the slicker. Blood seeped through the bandage Joshua had tied around her wound. "She doesn't look good." Clara touched her forehead. "No fever but I don't like seeing all that blood." Clara pulled the slicker closed. "Okay, you can turn back around."

"Weaver shot her. The bullet's still in there." Joshua felt her pulse. It was weaker. "I hope Doc Fisher gets here soon."

"Weaver won't be hurting anyone else. He died shortly after you left." Luke patted Joshua on the back. "We'll be praying. She's like a sister to me."

"Thank you." Joshua said as Luke left.

Clara lit another lamp. "Oh my." In the lamplight Anna's face was swollen and bruised. Her lips were cut, and she had blood around her mouth. There were scratches and bruises on her neck and chest. "I need to get her out of these clothes, clean her up and put a nightgown on her. What happened Joshua?"

"Weaver said he raped, beat and shot her. I don't know if he raped her, but she was obviously assaulted. Ben was no match for Weaver. He didn't have a chance." Joshua walked toward the door. "I don't know how I'll ever forgive myself for letting Anna get into this trouble. The only good news is that Weaver is dead."

"Joshua, you can't blame yourself for the monster that man was. He's dead. He can't hurt anyone else. She's going to need us. We can't help Ben, but I'm not going to let Anna go. Why don't you do some talking to Jesus while you put water on to heat? That will be better than kicking yourself for what you could've or should've done." Clara started unbuttoning the bloody dress, what was left of it.

~

Joshua woke when the door opened to Clara's room. He had taken a cue from Noah and slept on some blankets in the corner. "Sorry I dozed off when I was supposed to be helping you."

Clara sat down in a chair by the bed. "It's fine. I stayed in here and did some napping too. I went out for a few minutes to check on Ella and the kids. You had a hard day yesterday. Why don't you go to your bed? I'm fine here."

"I don't know what any of us would've done without you, Mother." Joshua raked his hand through his hair. "When did Doc Fisher say he'd be back?"

"He said around noon. The bullet's out. She has lots of bruises and cuts, but nothing was broken. We need to watch for signs of infection and fever. The loss of blood may have caused temporary unconsciousness. He doesn't think she hit her head. He didn't find any lumps. Get some sleep son, I'll wake you if anything changes." Clara straightened Anna's blanket.

"Okay, I can hardly keep my eyes open." Joshua stood up. "I can't help anyone like this. After I take a nap though, it's your turn. I'll help Ella with the children and keep an eye on Anna."

Chapter Seventeen

Anna heard a voice, but it sounded far away and she couldn't tell who it was. She forced herself to concentrate on the voice. Had Weaver found her? She chanced a look, but she only saw light.

She remembered her arm throbbing in pain after Weaver shot her and trying to hold onto the horse as he ran through the forest. She couldn't stop because Weaver might find her. She rode for hours until she fell out of the saddle. Then there was nothing.

Am I back at the cave? No. Please God, no!

When had she started talking to God? She'd asked God to help her escape. Her heart beat wildly, but she found the courage to open her eyes. Clara's face came into focus over her. She held her hand and asked Anna if she could hear her. Anna looked around the room. There was the dresser and the chair and the window under the oak tree. She was back at the ranch. Someone had found her. Clara whispered in her ear, "Our prayers have been answered," and squeezed her hand.

Relief washed over Anna and tears escaped from

the corners of her eyes. One after another slid down her cheeks. God had saved her. He'd given her another chance, even though she had doubted His existence and blamed Him for everything that had gone wrong in her life. He was there when she called out to Him.

Anna thanked Clara as she propped pillows behind her and gave her a drink of water. Pain shot through Anna's arm as she reached for the glass. Clara explained Doc Fisher got the bullet out of her arm. "You'll have to use your other arm until it heals. We're to watch for signs of infection" Clara left to tell everyone Anna was awake.

Yells of joy burst forth in the kitchen. Soon after the door opened and five children ran in. Joshua and Luke crowded in the small room. Clara carried Emily. A sea of faces looked down on her.

"We heard great news." Luke winked at Anna. "I see it's true. You had us pretty scared."

Ella hugged Anna on her good side. "I'm glad you're okay, Miss Wilson."

Joshua spoke from the foot of the bed. "Are you in much pain?"

"Only when I move my arm." Tears ran down Anna's cheeks. "I didn't know if I'd ever see any of you again."

"Hey, no crying or you'll have us tough cowboys doing the same." Luke looked at Jack and Noah while patting Anna's hand. "We can't ruin our reputation can we?"

"Nope, we cowboys don't cry." Noah took a step closer. "We sure are sorry Mr. Weaver hurt you."

Anna looked to Luke. "Is he alive? Where is he?"

"He won't be hurting anyone again. Where he's

gone, he'll be paying for all the hurt he caused." Luke squeezed Anna's hand. "Well, kids, I bet your father and Miss Wilson have some talking to do. Why don't we go to the barn and check on the kittens? They're chasing the puppies now."

As much as Anna appreciated seeing the faces of the people she'd come to love, she was grateful to be alone with Joshua. She had questions.

"Thank you Luke." Joshua patted him on the back as he followed the children out the door. "You can all come back later if Miss Wilson is up to it."

"I'm sure I will be. I want to hug all of you." Anna wiped tears from her eyes with her good hand.

Joshua sat in the chair next to Anna. "How do you really feel?"

"I hurt everywhere." Anna closed her eyes. It was hard to be this close to Joshua and not let him see how much he meant to her.

"Are you tired? We can talk later if you need to sleep." Joshua moved to get up.

"No, I'm fine. I need to know what happened. I need to know how Ben is. You did find him, right?" Anna looked at Joshua.

"Doc Fisher found him on his way to check on a family. That was some piece of good fortune. He stopped his bleeding and brought him here as fast as he could." Joshua reached over and held Anna's hand. "Ben didn't make it, Anna, but he helped us find you."

Her whole body shook from the waves of emotion pouring out of her. "He fell in my lap after Weaver shot him. His blood soaked into my skirt. I wanted to help him, but that monster wouldn't let me. He made me leave him on the wagon bench." Anna covered her face

144

with her hands and sobbed.

"Try to calm down, Anna, you've been through a lot. You're right, Ben didn't deserve to die. Jack and Noah didn't deserve to live with a man like that, either. And you didn't deserve what he did to you."

"There are evil people with no conscience, and they don't care what they do or who they hurt. If it hadn't been that day, then it would've been another, or if it hadn't been Ben, it might have been someone else or maybe the children. We don't know why it went bad now. You have to believe, it wasn't you, anyone else or God who was responsible. It was Weaver and the awful choices he made. I'll miss Ben a lot, we all will, but you can't blame yourself." Joshua leaned over and pushed strands of hair dampened by her tears back from her face.

Anna wondered why Joshua was being so comforting. "Did I kill Weaver?"

"He was alive when we found him in the cave, but I knew he wouldn't last much longer. I left Luke and a couple of the men with him. Steven and I followed your trail, but it was getting dark. We had to stop because we couldn't see the horse's tracks any longer."

"After we dismounted, I heard a horse nicker. I found you lying on the ground next to the horse. God must have kept him there so we would be able to find you." Joshua ran his hand over his two day beard. "When I saw you lying there, I thought you were dead, Anna. My heart nearly broke. I thought I'd never get a chance to make things right with you."

Anna twisted the tie on the top of her nightgown. "There's nothing you need to make right Joshua. You've always been honest with me."

"When I found you, your dressed was ripped to shreds." Joshua bent his head and when he looked up, his eyes glistened with unshed tears. "I'm sorry I didn't protect you."

Anna saw intense sorrow in Joshua's blue eyes. She shuddered as memories of Weaver assaulting her came flooding back. She told Joshua what happened in the cave.

"I was so scared and trembling from head to toe. I asked God to help me, and somehow I knew He would. I stopped trembling immediately and knew what I had to do. He didn't rape me, Joshua, but I feel so dirty. I have never hated anyone, but I hated him. I killed him and I'm not sorry. Shouldn't I be sad I took a man's life? How can I live with all this hate and anger?" Anna turned her head away.

"Anna, look at me. I want you to know I'm sincere. You had to stop him. In fact, I consider you a hero. Who knows how many children and women he would've hurt if you hadn't stopped him. I'm the one who should feel guilty for not being there to protect you. I should've realized he wouldn't give up without getting revenge." Joshua continued looking into Anna's eyes. "I think the important thing here is that we both know that God listens when we pray."

"I knew I was going to die if God didn't help me. Do you think He gave me the strength to do what I had to do?" Anna smiled.

"I do." Joshua said as he took her hand in his.

Clara knocked and stepped into the room. "Doc Fisher is here to check on Anna."

Joshua let go of Anna's hand and stood up as the doctor walked in.

Doc Fisher sat his bag at the bottom of the bed. "Well now, this is a much happier state of affairs. I'm happy to return to good news this time. Let's check that bullet wound."

Chapter Eighteen

"Why are we packing our bags, Miss Wilson?" Ella sat beside the suitcase on her bed.

Anna folded Ella's dress and laid it neatly on top of her other clothes. "Luke went to Nacogdoches for me to purchase train tickets. We're going back to New York City." She closed the bag and fixed the buckles.

Ella wrung her hands. "I want to live here. This is the first home I've known since I went to the orphanage."

"I'm sorry, Ella. I wish we could stay here, but Miss Clara has help I insisted she get. Luke promised not to say anything to Miss Clara or Mr. Brown. I plan on telling them at dinner. Anna drew Ella into her arms. We knew when we left New York City, there was always the possibility we would return. I understand you love it here, and I feel bad taking you back to the orphanage, but the orphanage won't be forever. I have a plan. I'm going to get my teaching certificate and as soon as I have a position somewhere, hopefully in the west, we will go there together." Anna pushed one of

Ella's red curls back out of her eyes and dried her tears. "I want you to be with me forever, Ella."

"I want that too, Miss Wilson. I just wish it could be here." Ella blew her nose on the hanky Anna offered her. She was such a brave girl. "I'm going to see if Miss Clara needs help with dinner." Ella closed the bedroom door behind her as she left.

Anna sat on Ella's bed. She didn't want to leave either, but she had to. She wasn't needed at the ranch anymore. Besides, it had been six weeks since she was shot, and her arm was healing well. Even Jack and Noah had found a home and didn't need her. They went to live with the Carson's. Her frequent trips to the Carson's farm assured her the boys had found a very good home, and Anna had found a very good friend in Beth. It felt like she'd known her for years instead of a few months.

Everything seemed settled except her. Almost every night she had nightmares about Weaver. She woke up with her heart pounding and her skin wet with sweat. She prayed until her heart returned to its natural rhythm and she went back to sleep. She prayed for a day when all the things Weaver had done to the boys, to Ben, and to her would be less painful but she didn't see that happening anytime soon. And there was the regret she lived with daily. She shouldn't have left the ranch with Ben that day. Every day she was reminded of her impatience. His sister, Megan, had come from Dallas for the funeral and decided to stay on at the ranch. She helped Clara with the cleaning and cooking. Although Megan had never blamed Anna for Ben's death, Anna felt responsible.

Leaving Clara would be especially hard. She was

the gift Anna had never expected. She filled a big part of the hole left when her mother died. She had missed having someone to talk to. Anna and Clara spoke about every subject but one, Joshua.

He was the real reason she couldn't stay at the ranch. Anna could no longer deny, at least to herself, that she loved him. The last six weeks while she'd been healing from everything, he'd been kind, helpful and attentive. How could she not love him?

She'd been attracted to Joshua since her first day in Nacogdoches, when she landed on top of him at the train depot. They didn't always agree, but as she watched him with the children, she saw how different he was from anyone she'd ever known.

Her so-called love for Bennett had been nothing but an infatuation, a young girl's first love. She'd never go back to him, no matter how bad things got in New York City. She hoped he had changed and could now be a good father. His children needed him.

Ella opened the door and peeked in. "Miss Wilson, dinner is ready."

Anna followed Ella downstairs. She wasn't looking forward to telling everyone they'd be leaving. Clara would try to talk her out of it, and Ella would be giving her the puppy dog eyes from across the table.

Clara sat a bowl of potatoes on the table and motioned for Anna to sit next to her. "How was your nap?"

"I didn't end up sleeping at all." Anna sat down.

Joshua walked into the dining room with Luke. "I asked Luke to join us tonight. I want to talk to him about improvements we need to make to the ranch before winter hits." Joshua sat across form Anna and smiled warmly at her. Anna looked at her hands in her lap.

"You're not going to talk about that at dinner, are you?" Clara's raised brow spoke volumes.

Joshua chuckled, "No, Mother, I know better."

"Well, good, why don't you pray and we can eat?" Clara winked at her son.

Anna pushed the food around on her plate but only took a couple of bites. She feared she would throw up from the stress of keeping her near departure a secret. Luke watched her, he gave her an encouraging nod. Only he knew what she was going to say. At first, he'd argued with her about buying the tickets, pressing her to talk to Joshua about her decision to leave. In the end, Luke had done what she had asked of him, even though he didn't want to keep things from Joshua.

Anna couldn't put announcing her leaving off any longer. She swallowed hard before she spoke. "Excuse me, I need to let everyone know Ella and I will be leaving in two days to go back to New York City. I'm sorry I didn't say anything until now, but it's so hard to leave. With Megan here to help Clara, this is the best decision for everyone. The children are and always have been very well taken care of. I must apologize for my doubts at the beginning. Ella and I have loved being here. You've become like family to us, but we can't impose on you any longer. We'll miss you all so much."

"You can't be serious about leaving. Megan is here to help us, not take your place. This family and house has more than enough work for ten of us and the other two women Joshua talked to decided they didn't want to work here." Clara patted Anna's hand and chuckled.

"I'm sorry, but I already have our tickets. Please, excuse me." Anna got up and ran through the kitchen and out the back door. The sun was setting, casting an orange glow over the summer browned grass. A chill rose goose bumps on her arms. She should've grabbed her sweater. Tears rolled down her cheeks as she looked around at all she would miss.

Joshua rushed down the porch steps toward her. "Why didn't you tell me you were leaving?"

"This hasn't been an easy decision." Anna wiped away her tears. "For heaven's sake, all I do around you is cry. I'm sorry I didn't say anything. Just know that Ella and I will be all right. You don't have to worry about us."

Joshua's voice came from a deep place. "If I asked you to stay, would you?" He laid his hand on her shoulder.

Anna flinched. Memories of Weaver touching her flooded her mind. The world spun. She bent over, breathed deeply, hoping to stop the spinning, but lost her balance. Joshua caught her. "You're always saving me from falling. First from an abandoned bag and now from my memories."

Joshua drew Anna up and held her steady. He guided her to the bench, and they sat down.

"I'm sorry my touch startled you. I wish you didn't have memories to battle."

"My mind spends too much time on memories of Weaver, whether I'm awake or asleep. Your touch is nothing like Weavers, nothing at all. He was savage, and you are kind." Anna hid her face in her hands and sobbed.

Joshua reached up and gently pulled her hands

away. "I need you to look at me Anna. You must know that I would never hurt you. I should have said something sooner. I didn't want to overwhelm you with all I wanted to say. I had hoped you would see through my actions, but I realize now I shouldn't have waited so long."

"You don't have to apologize. I've been doing a lot of thinking and praying. When I first came here, you probably hoped I would leave for New York City that day and not look back. A lot has happened, but we knew I would indeed need to return to the city and the orphanage." A whinny drew Anna's attention to the corral. Tornado pranced and kicked around his mother. She would never forget the night he was born.

Joshua stood and held his hand out to Anna. "Can we go for a walk? I talk better when I walk."

Anna stood. She slipped her hand out of his. He didn't resist but smiled warmly at her. He led her to the creek where the water slid gently over the rocky bottom. He offered a hand to help her onto a flat boulder at the creek's shore.

"I was about ten when I started coming here to plan my future. I never dreamed I'd still be living here doing the same things my father did. It's funny how life goes."

Anna closed her eyes and lifted her face to the setting sun. The rock was warm to her touch, the chill of evening had not yet cooled it. The soft song of the water trickling over the rocks soothed her. The peace of the place reminded her of her childhood hiding place.

"There was a dead tree which had fallen on the back of our property. It had been a big tree, so it made the perfect place to sit or lay on. The breeze blew the leaves, and the sun's rays warmed me, just like the sun is doing today. That tree was where I dreamed of how my life would be."

Joshua laid his hand on top of hers. "What were those dreams Anna?"

Anna didn't flinch at his touch. "Oh, the usual girl dreams. I dreamed of marrying the most handsome prince and living in a big stone castle, the kind I'd seen in story books. That prince and I had lots of beautiful children, who knew they were always loved." Anna met Joshua's gaze. "My dreams didn't turn out quite how I'd hoped."

"Your life isn't over yet. I can't offer you a castle, and I am certainly no prince, but sometime during the last few months I've fallen in love with you, Anna. I tried to deny it to myself because I didn't want to betray Sarah's memory. I tried to keep my distance after our first kiss the night Tornado was born, but some irresistible force kept pulling me to you. And truthfully, I was worried because you were so bitter toward God. I hoped someday you would forgive Him, but I couldn't take that risk.

"I'm afraid that my actions were often different from my words. I didn't understand why God would bring you here when there wasn't a future for us. My thoughts and feelings were in conflict over what I should do or say to you on a daily basis. When you told me you'd made peace with God, I started to hope we could have a future together.

"I'm amazed by your strength, Anna." Joshua wrapped his fingers in hers. "I don't want to rush you or make you feel you should already love me. I haven't made it easy for you. I hope you will stay here and see if maybe you can love me. I promise to court you the way a man should. Please think carefully about this. It would make me and my children very happy if you would stay and give me, us, a chance."

Anna couldn't believe the words Joshua was saying. How could he love her? She'd told him all the horrible things she'd done. He knew about Bennett and all that Weaver had done. Anna watched the water on its lazy course past the boulder. A leaf floated along with the current, not letting the obstacles stop its progress. Could a life with Joshua make them both happy? As Joshua held her hand, Anna realized that, like the leaf, she would get past the memories of Weaver. Joshua's touch calmed her fears and gave her strength.

Anna held his gaze. In his eyes she saw his love for her. "I don't need a prince or a castle. I don't need time or courting to know if I can love you. I already do. I think I first loved you when I woke up from the wagon accident, and your head was laying by me and you were holding my hand. I tried to hide my feelings because I didn't want your pity. Besides, you said you'd never marry again."

"I don't want you to regret asking me to stay. You should know now that I've promised Ella we'd be together forever. She's become a daughter to me. We would come as a package deal. And think carefully, also, if you would want a woman like me raising your children. I don't want you to regret asking me to stay." Anna put her hand over her racing heart as she waited for Joshua's answer.

"There isn't a better example of a mother than you, Anna. You've cared for countless children in the orphanage, and then on the orphan trains. They weren't a job for you but children who mattered. You even took me to task." Joshua chuckled. "Your love didn't stop there. You've cared for Ella, my children, and then Jack and Noah. Your love knows no bounds. The mistakes you made were just that, mistakes, and we've all made them.

"What Weaver did and tried to do to you was because he was evil. Your only guilt was in holding him accountable for the way he fathered those children. And that's no guilt at all. You did what you had to do.

"I want you and Ella to live here. Luke would never forgive me if I let you go. I'm a little jealous of the ease you two have with each other. He's assured me you are like a sister to him and nothing more."

Anna shook her head. "Joshua, you have nothing to worry about where Luke's concerned. He's the big brother I never had. She squeezed his hand. My heart knows only you. The thought of leaving here, of leaving you, shattered my heart. Instead, I'm hearing words from you I never dared to dream." Anna looked into the eyes of the man she loved without masking her feelings. She could love him with the assurance he would protect her love with his life.

"I've even considered building a home on the ranch where we take care of children who've lost their parents until they find new families to love them. I want us to dream and do things that will matter. Our strength comes from God and the three of us can accomplish more than we'd ever hoped." Joshua brushed her hair back from her face.

"I would love to help children who have lost everything and everyone. We could make such a difference if we did that. Children wouldn't be out on the streets trying to find a way to survive or forced into doing things they didn't want to. They wouldn't be in situations where they were treated badly. Who knows what we might accomplish and how many lives we'd make better. I love you even more for understanding what my desire has always been. I want to make a difference in the lives of children." Anna hugged Joshua.

Joshua rose and helped Anna to join him. He kissed her hand. I want to spend the rest of my life with you. "Will you marry me Anna? The sooner the better. I don't want to waste any more time not being able to hold you in my arms. I hope we'll have more children who look just like their beautiful mother." Joshua caressed Anna's cheek.

"I'll marry you and is tomorrow soon enough? I don't need a big wedding, just you." The only tears in Anna's eyes were tears of joy.

"Tomorrow would be great for me, but I have a feeling my mother won't let us get by without some type of wedding. She'll probably make us wait a week or two and she knows how to get her way." Joshua laughed. He moved his hand to the back of Anna's neck and massaged the tension from her muscles. "I remember well our first kiss. That kiss shook my world, and it needed some shaking. Can I kiss you again, Anna?"

Joshua leaned toward Anna, and she didn't feel any panic.

"Yes." Thoughts of Weaver never crossed her mind when the gentleness of Joshua's kiss left her breathless. This man loved her. She wrapped her arms around his neck and waited. She wasn't disappointed as Joshua's lips caressed hers again. Her heart found a home in the love of a Savior who never gave up on her and in the arms of a man who saw past her flaws and embraced her heart.

The End

Made in the USA
San Bernardino, CA
24 August 2017